For my seven year old self

Pansy Boy

Written and illustrated by Paul Harfleet

BARB ICAN PRESS

With eyes of green and curls of brown

He was a boy from an average town

He loved to draw and he loved to write, he marvelled at all things in flight

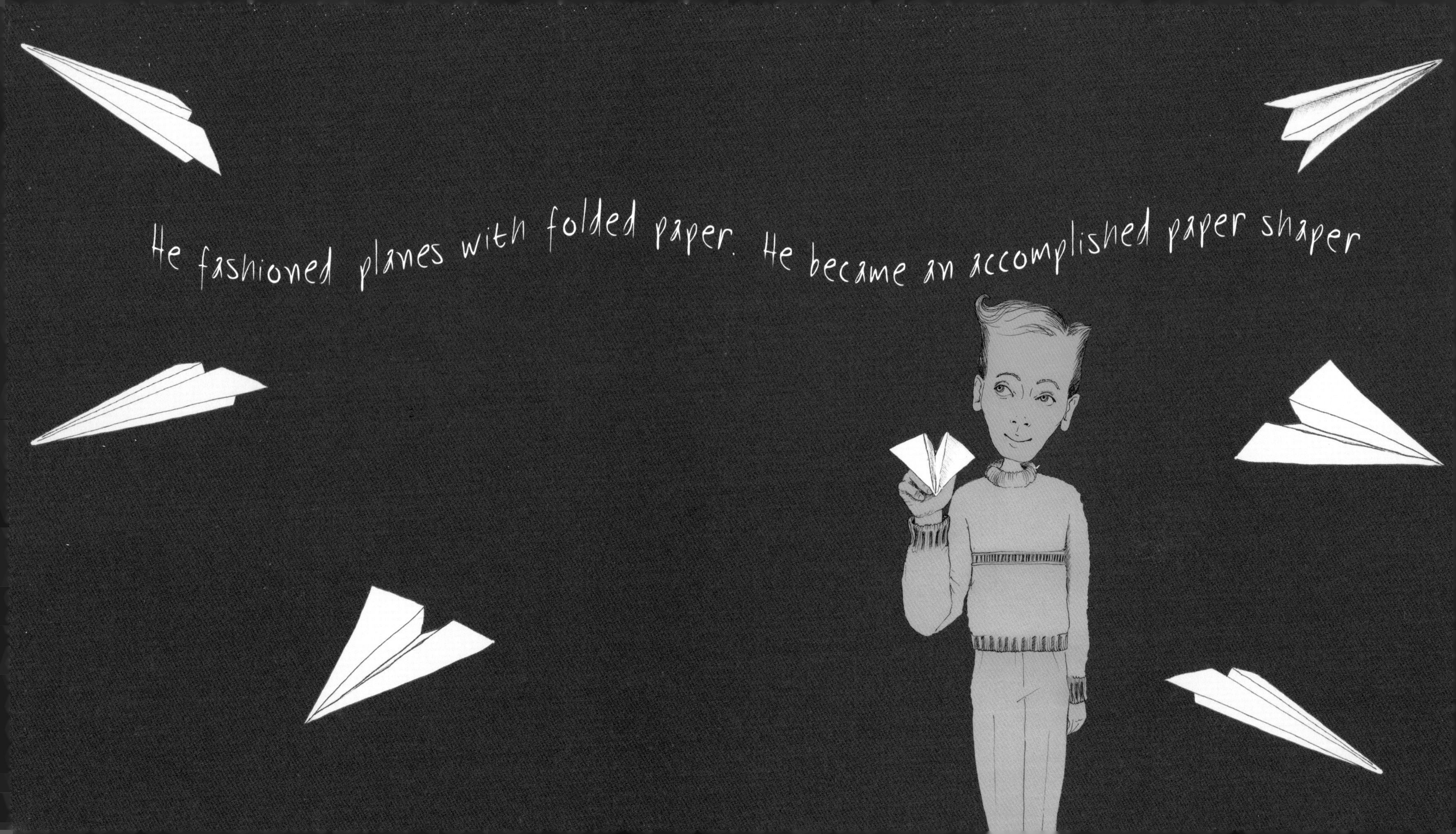

He fashioned planes with folded paper. He became an accomplished paper shaper

As birds flew by, he learned to love. Kestrel, lapwing, collared dove

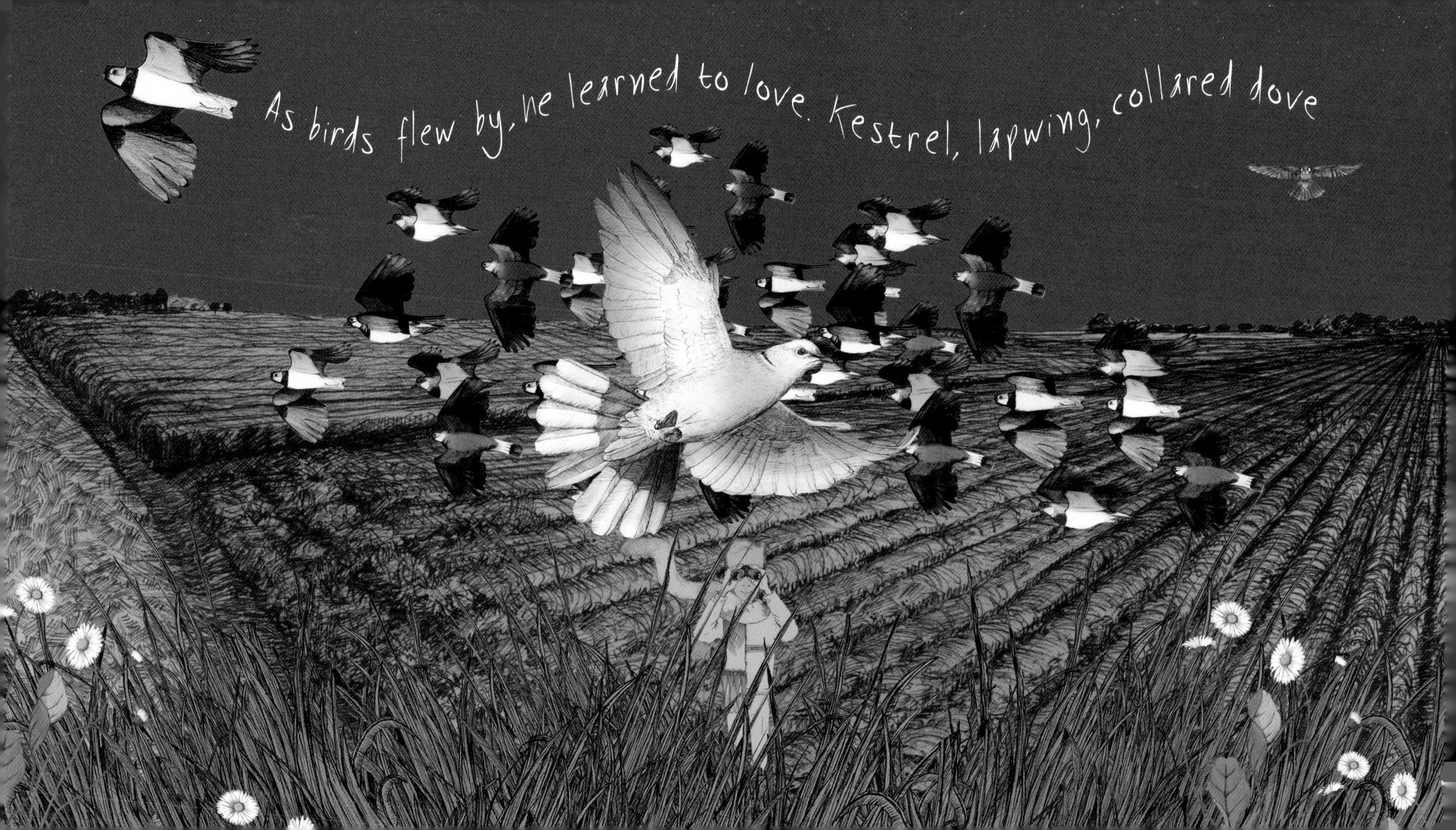

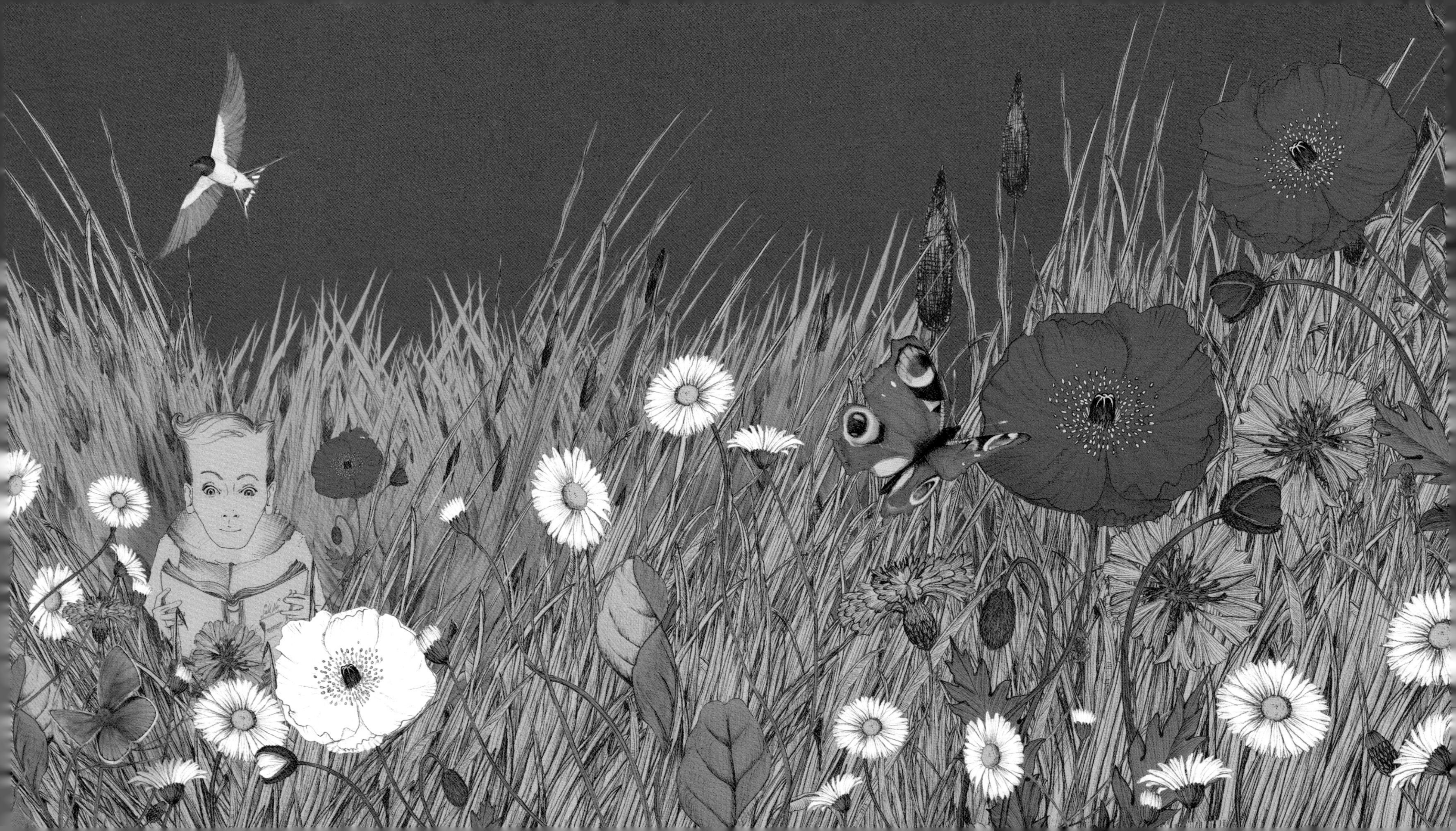

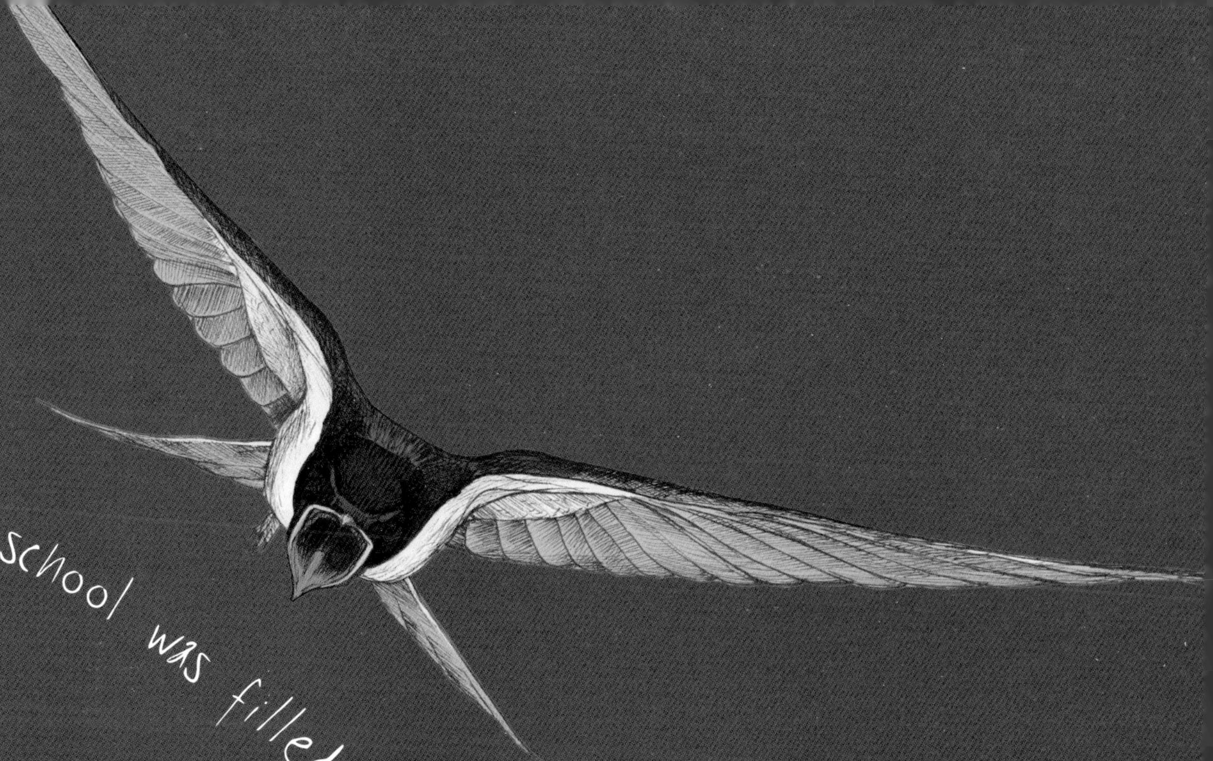

Holidays passed in reverie but school was filled with jeopardy

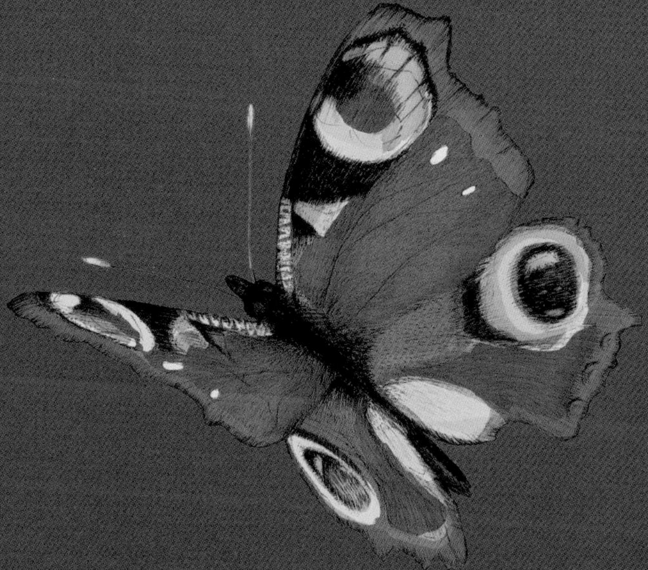

Slightly crestfallen and reluctantly glum
The day arrived that he knew would come
He packed up his satchel and pencil case
Put on his blazer and bravest face

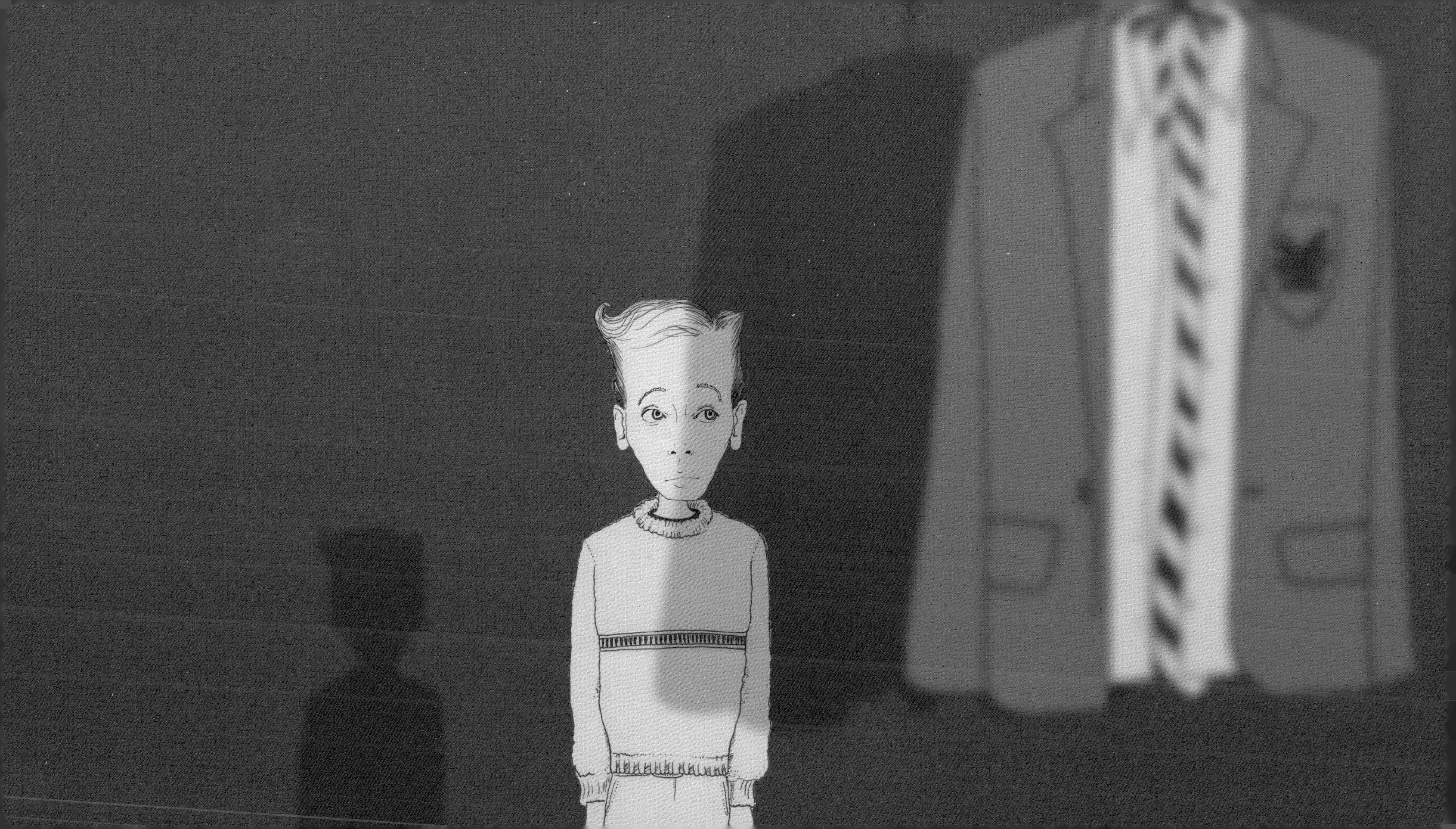

His stance and demeanour may have been fey
His nature girlish and potentially gay

It's not as though he had a say
It was always clear he was born this way

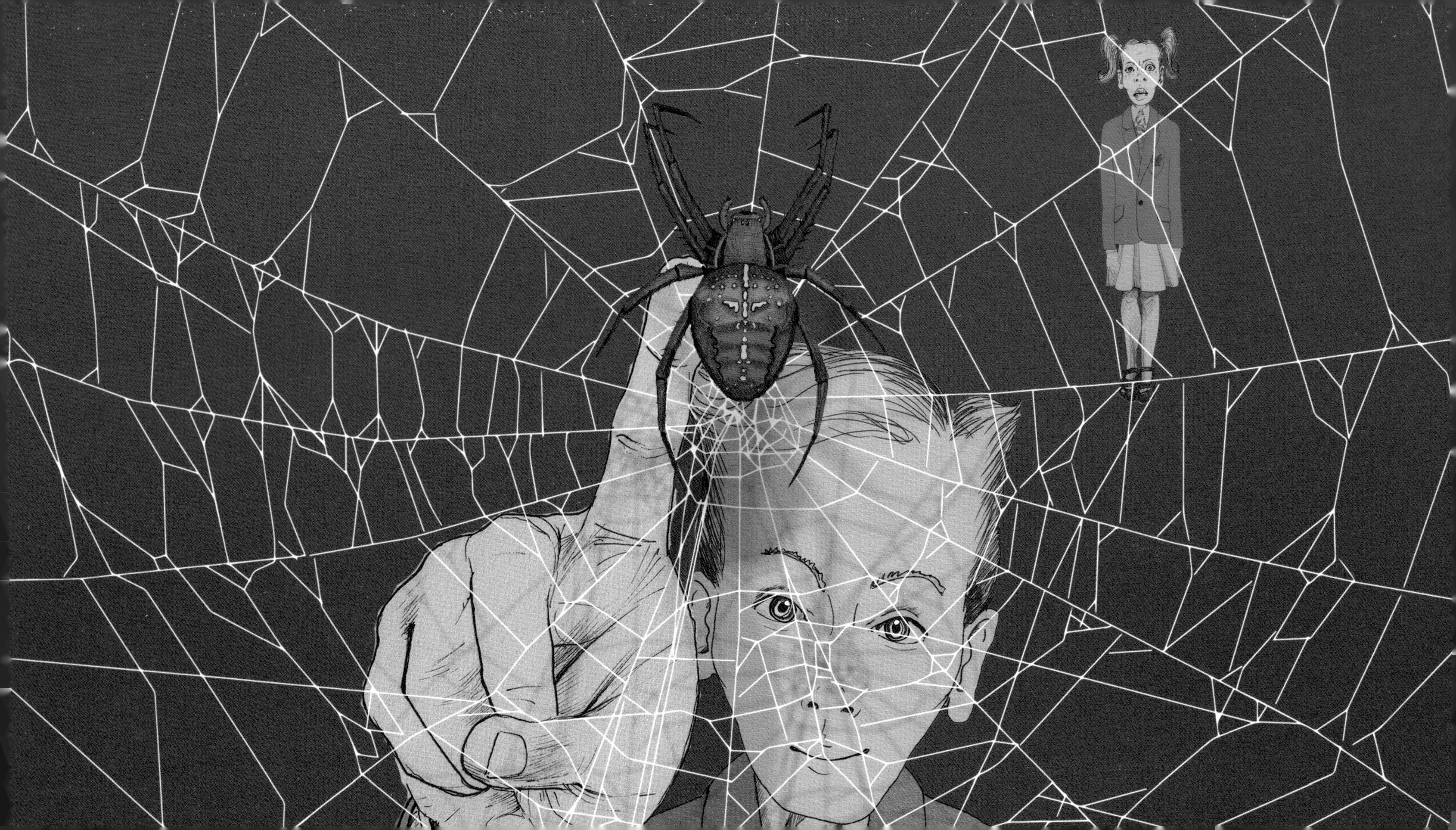

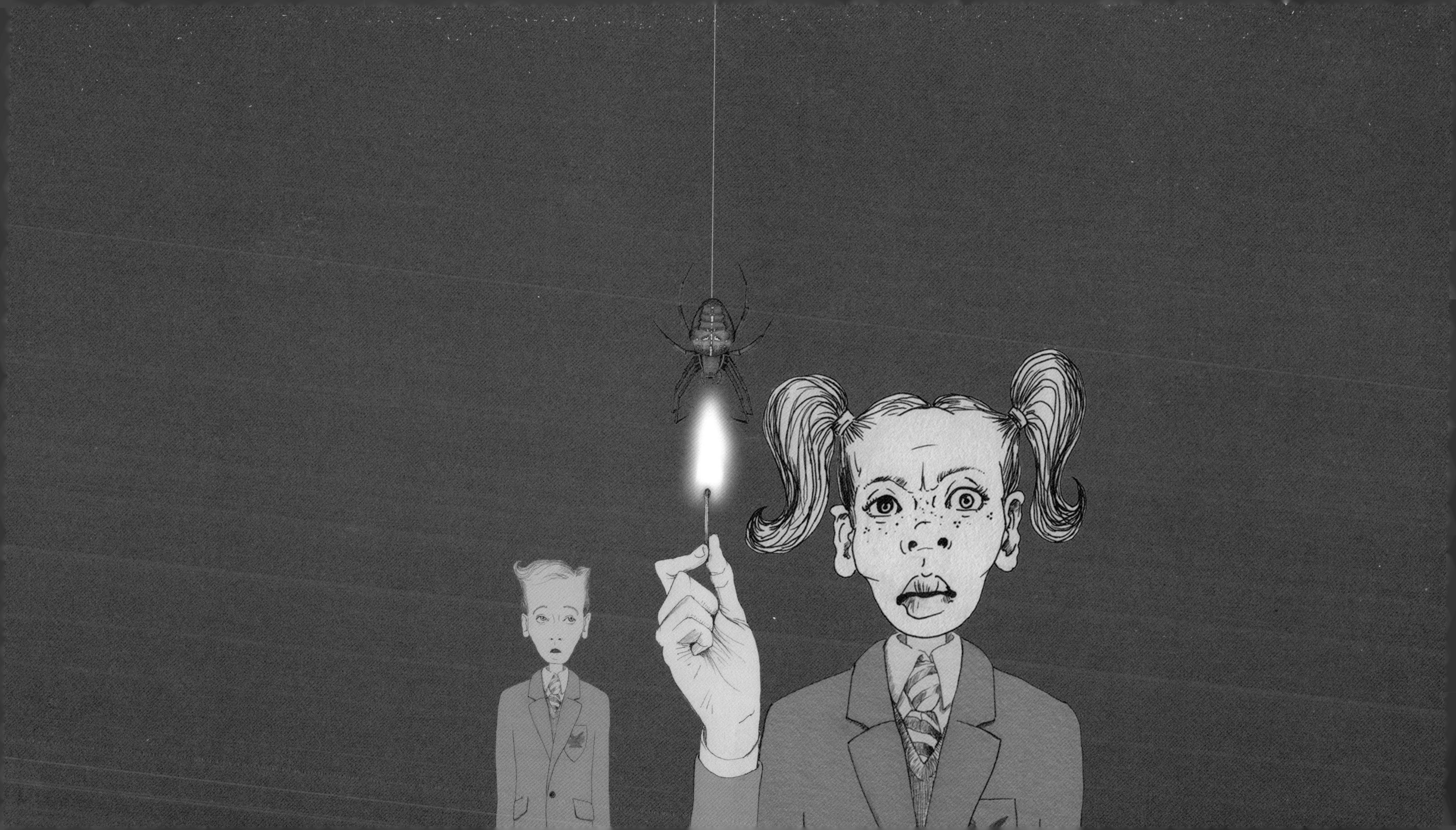

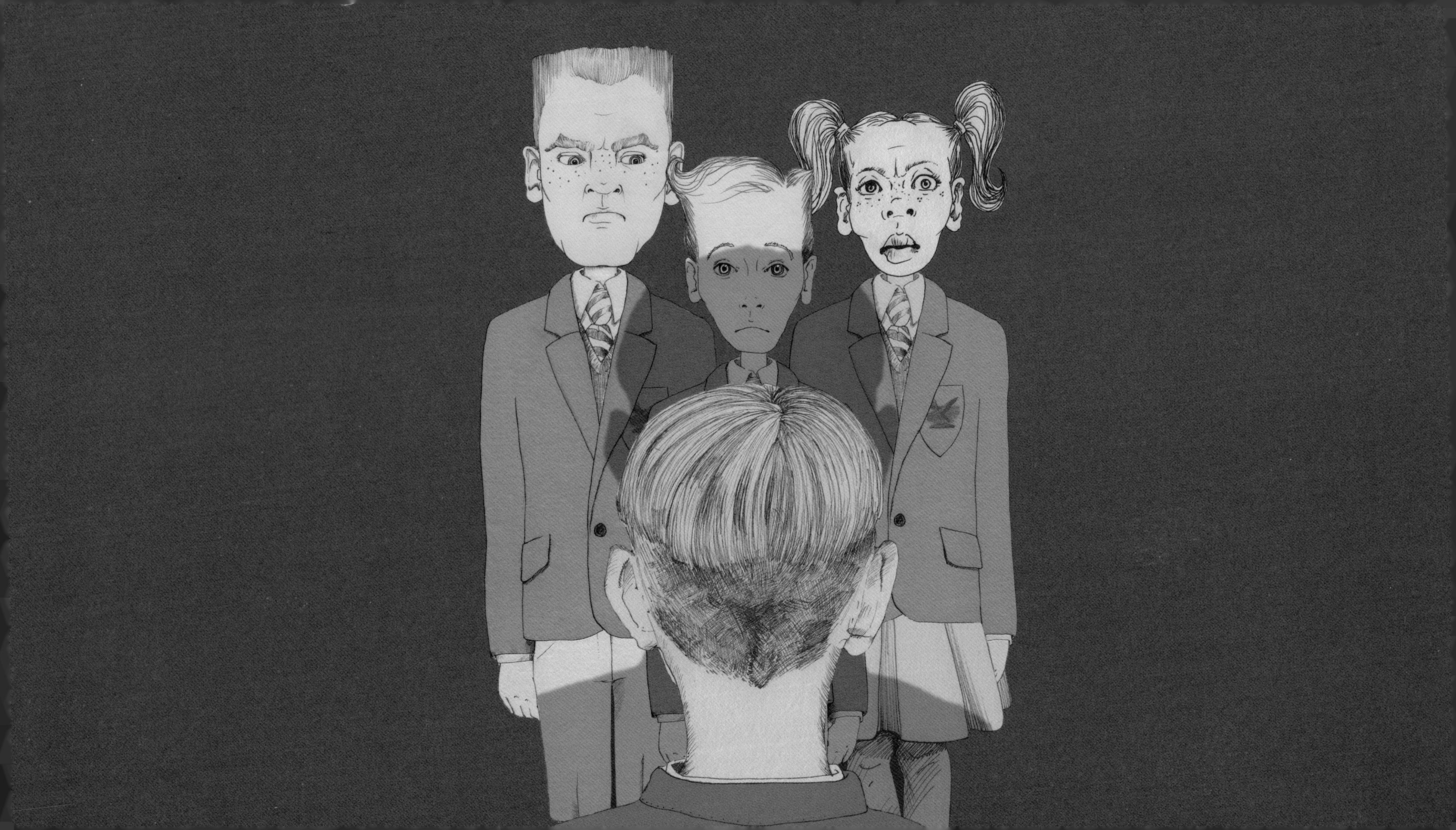

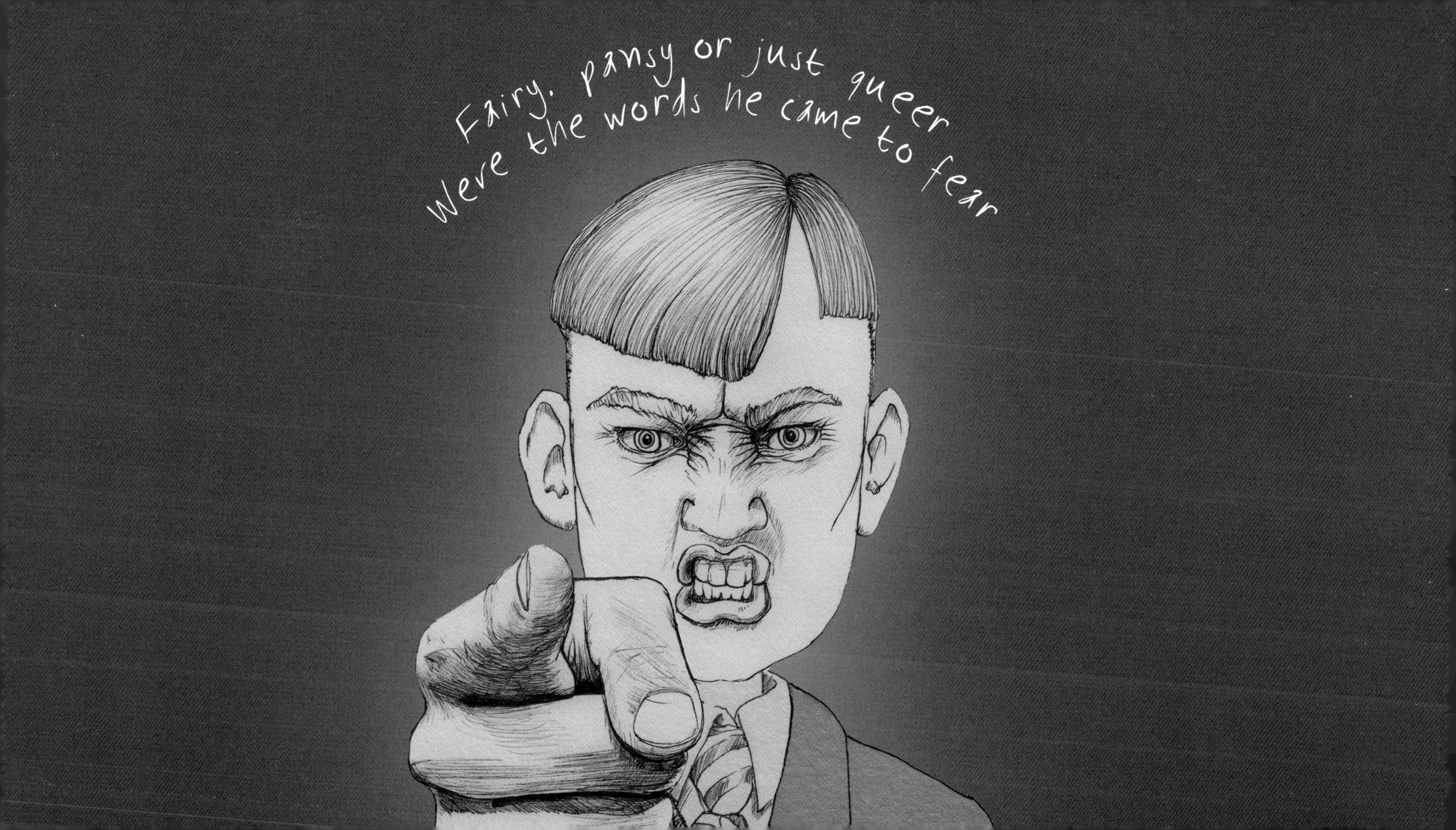
Fairy, pansy or just queer
Were the words he came to fear

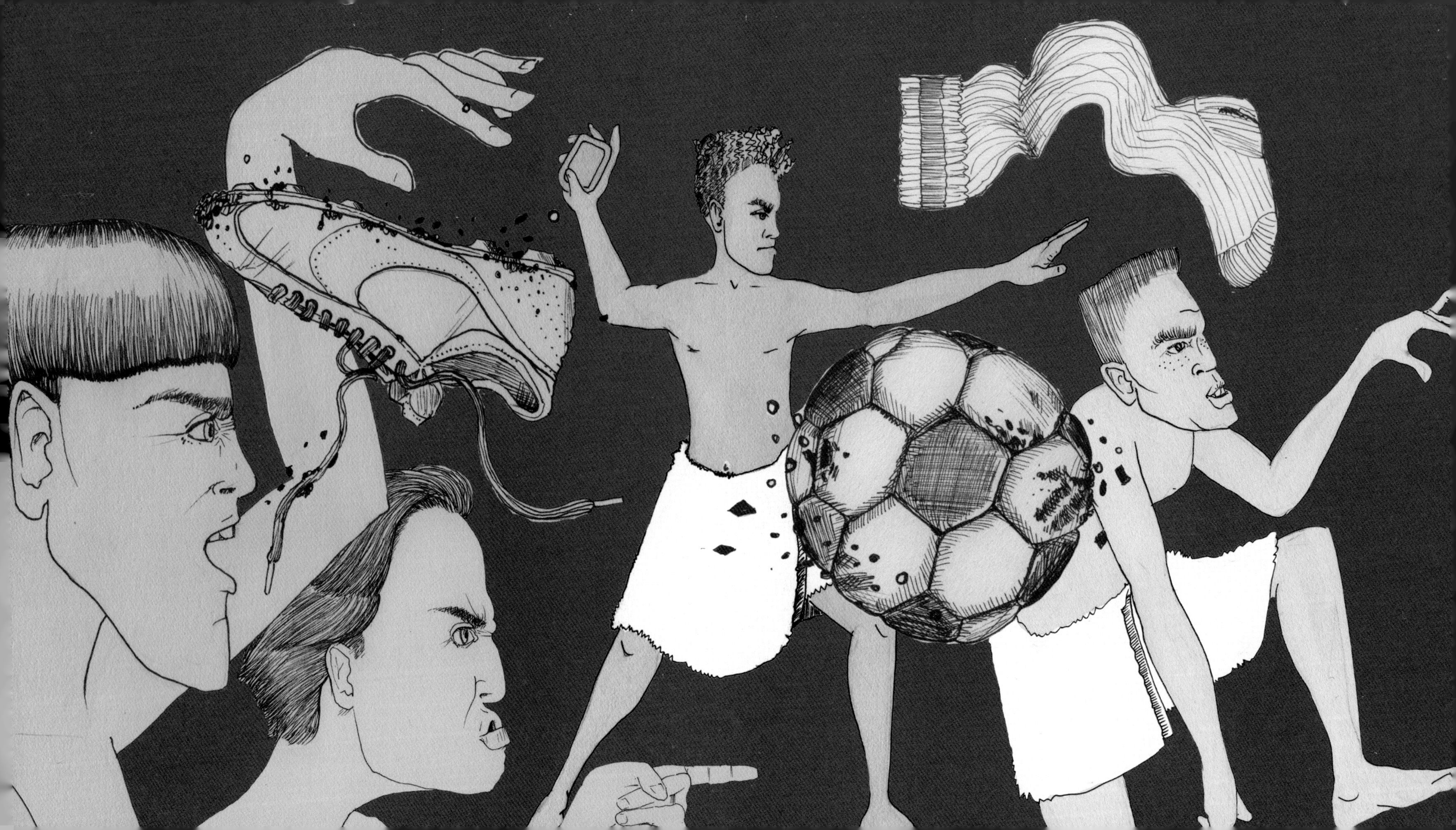

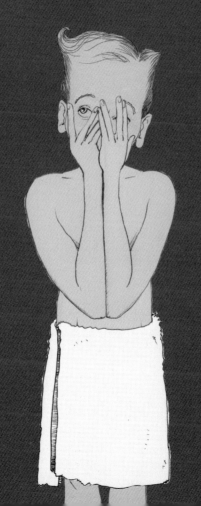

From dawn till dusk
he dealt with the plight
Of schoolboy tyrants
filled with spite

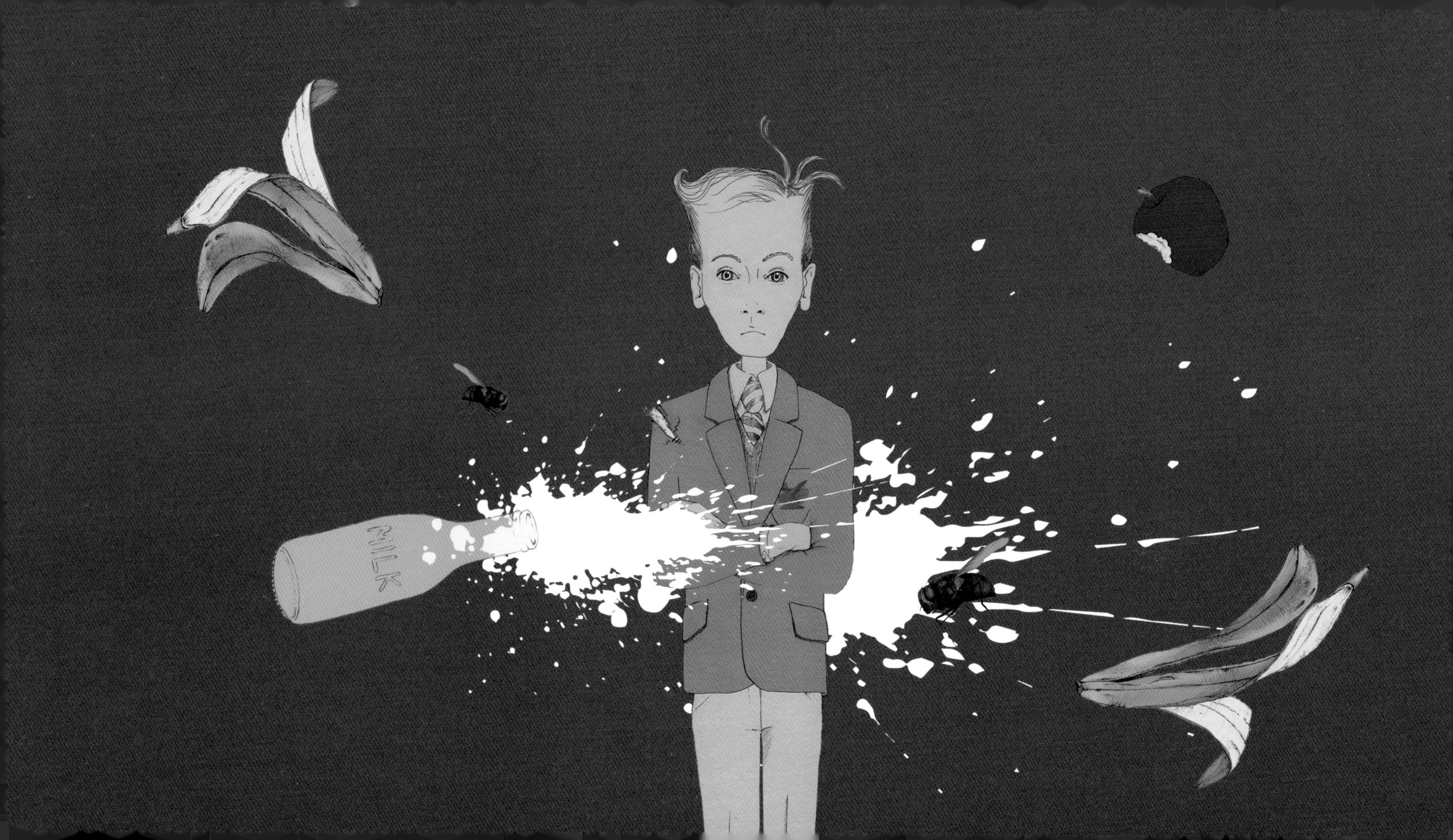
MILK

He refused to be bullied for the rest of the year
He had to conquer the cause of his fear

He'd find a way to rise above
Those that bully shout and shove

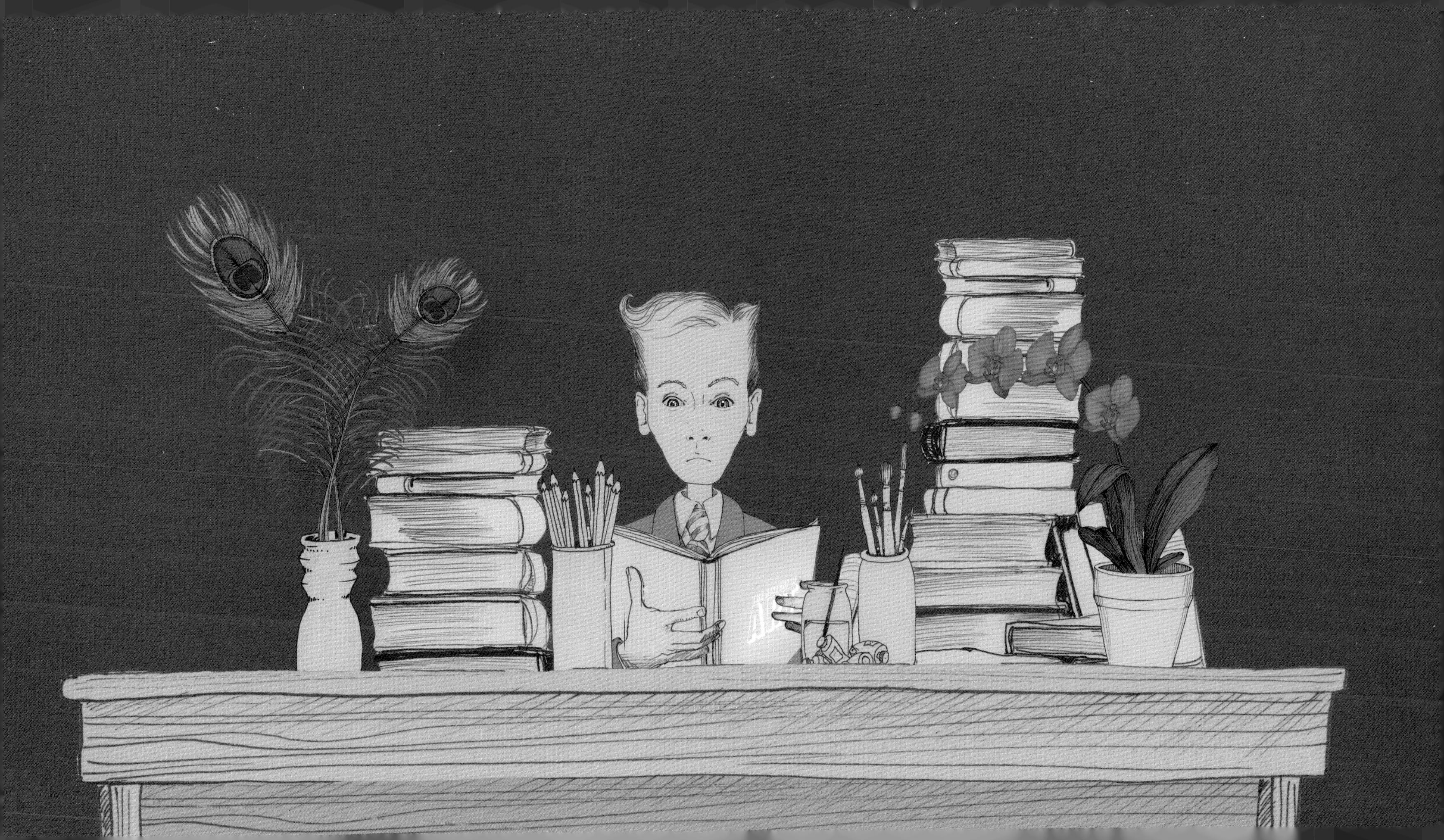

He worked so hard to strategize, he needed to sleep to rest his eyes
He hoped his dreams could generate, a simple plan to tackle the hate

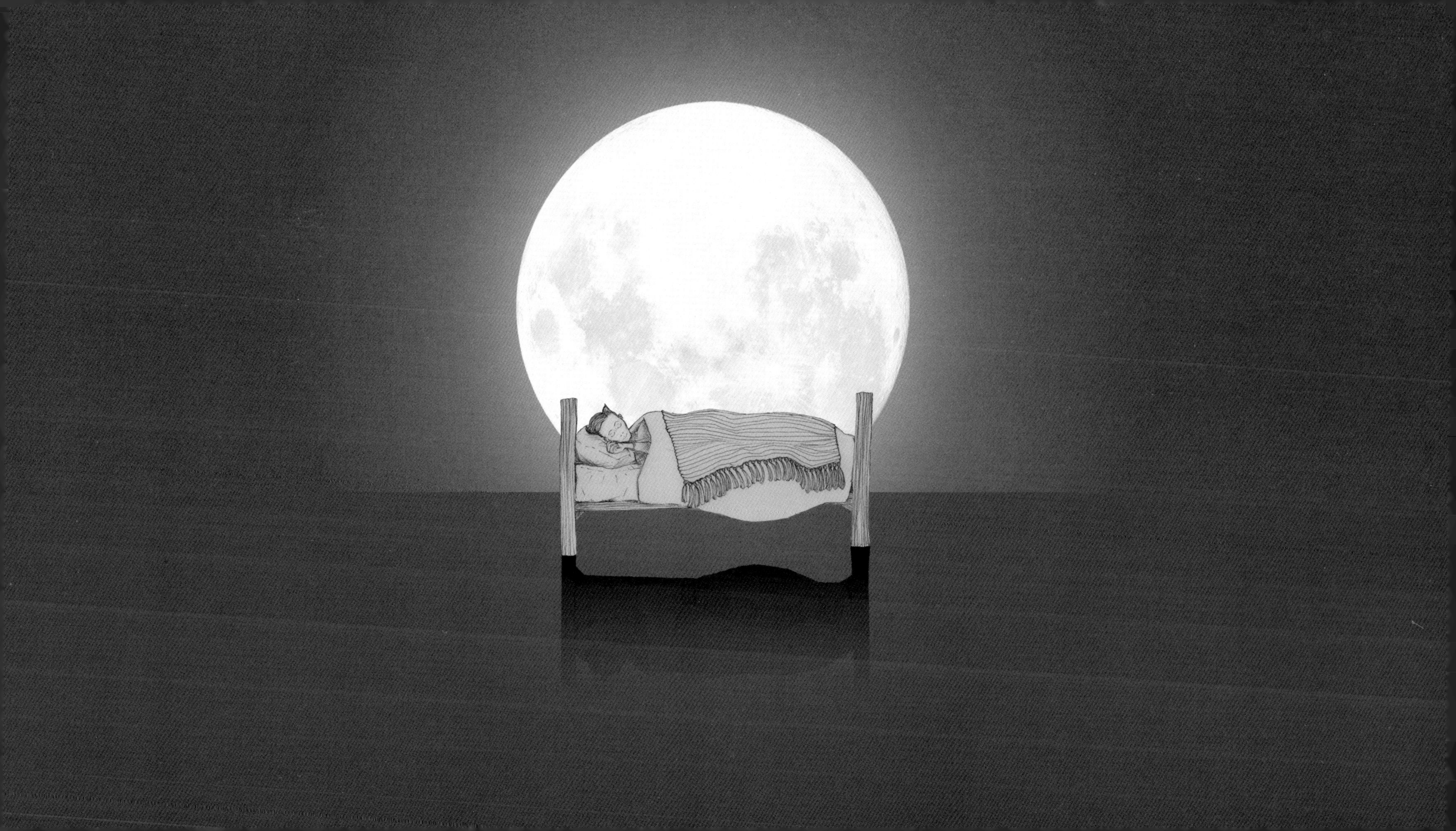

In the morning with increasing pace

He went in search of a thinking space

He found a bike, adorned with flowers

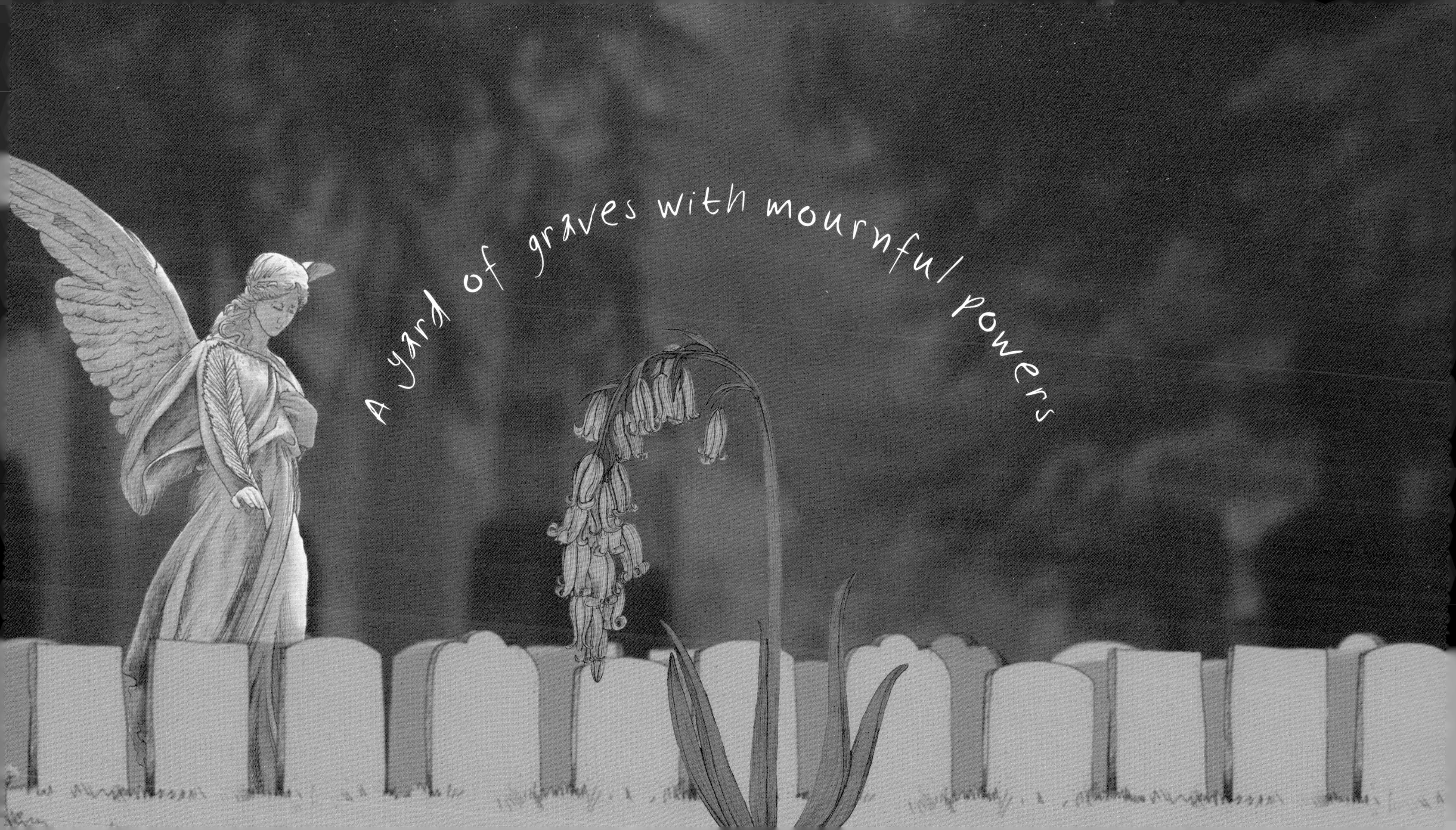
A yard of graves with mournful powers

In locations layered with human woe

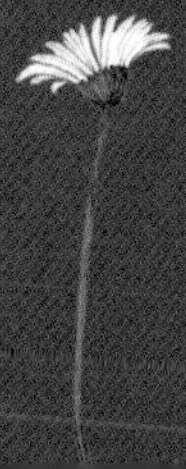

He found an idea that began to grow

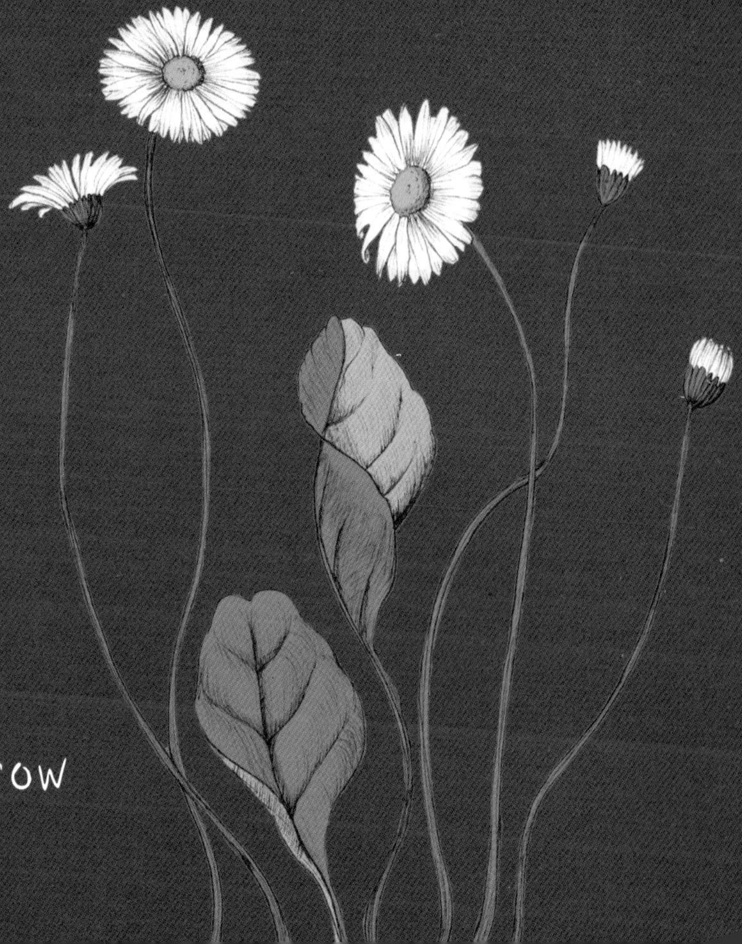

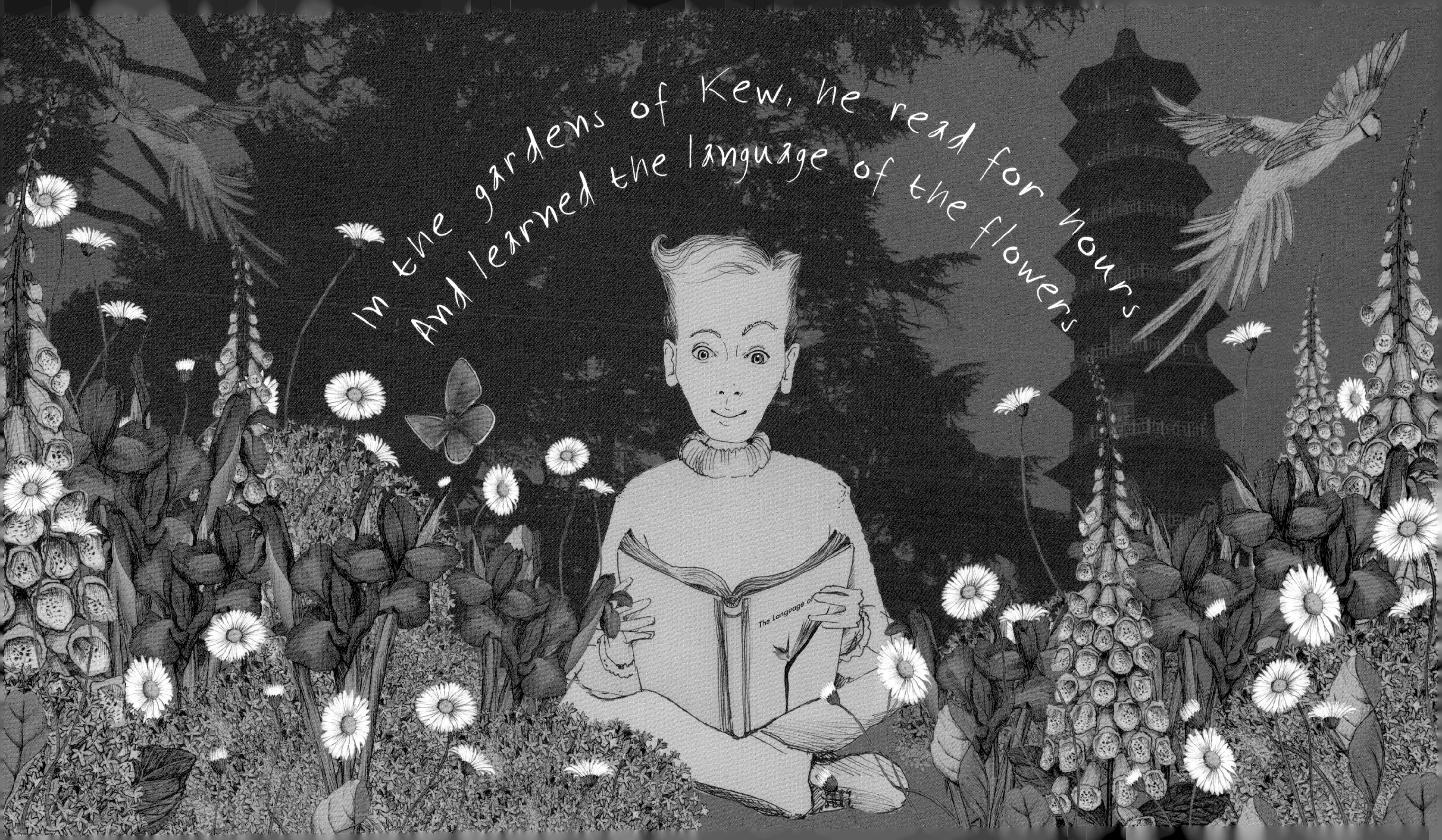
The Language of

In the gardens of Kew, he read for hours
And learned the language of the flowers

The science of plants cultivated by man

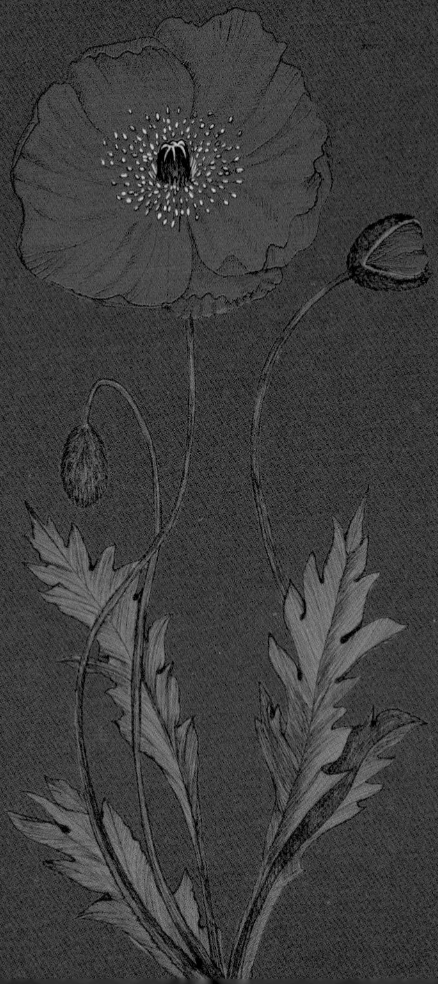

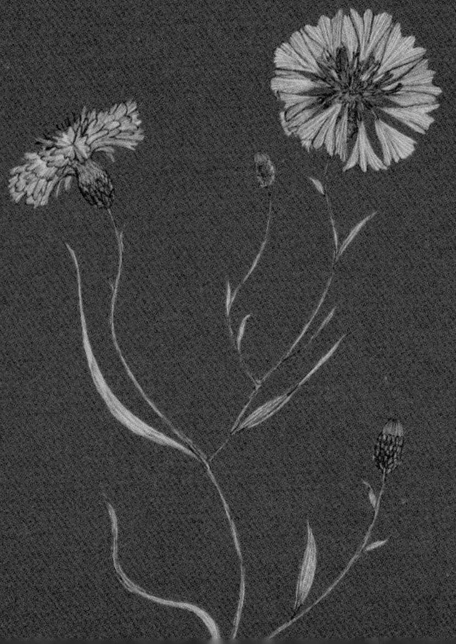

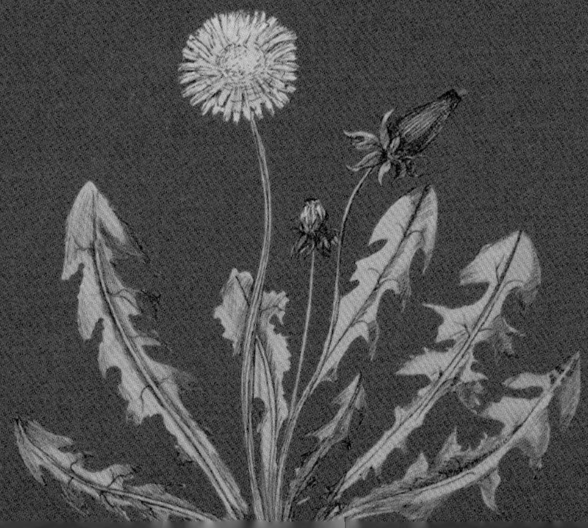

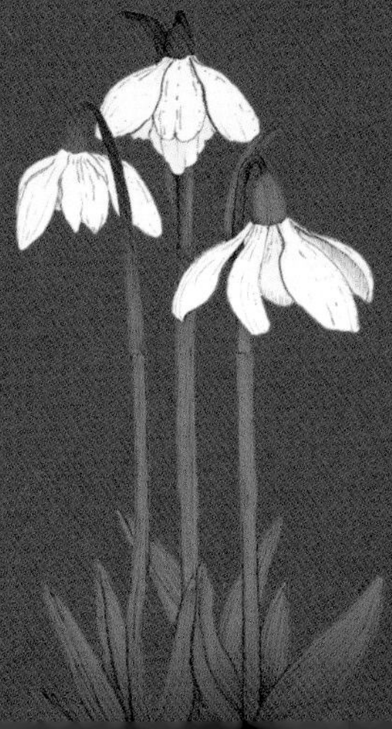

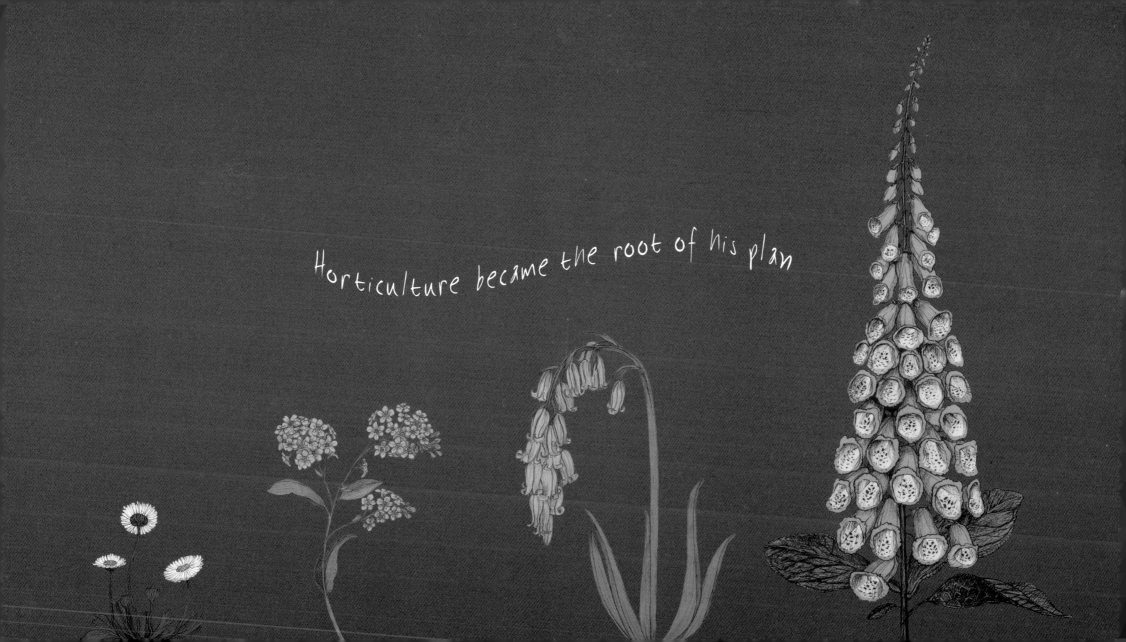

Horticulture became the root of his plan

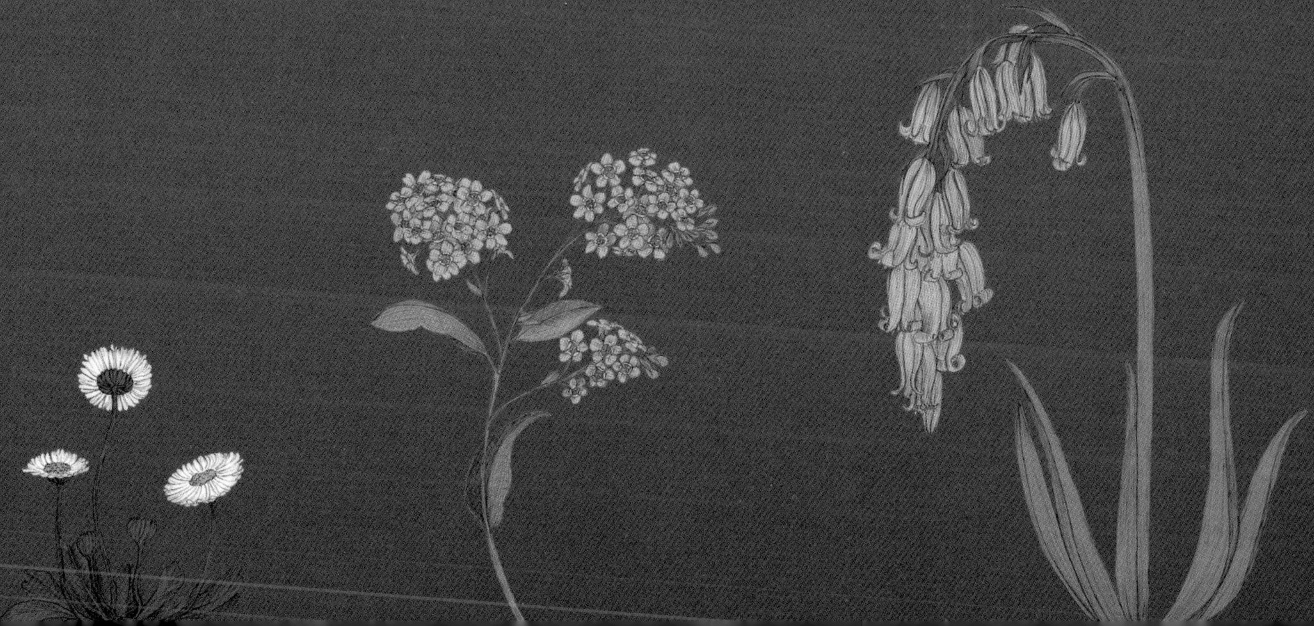

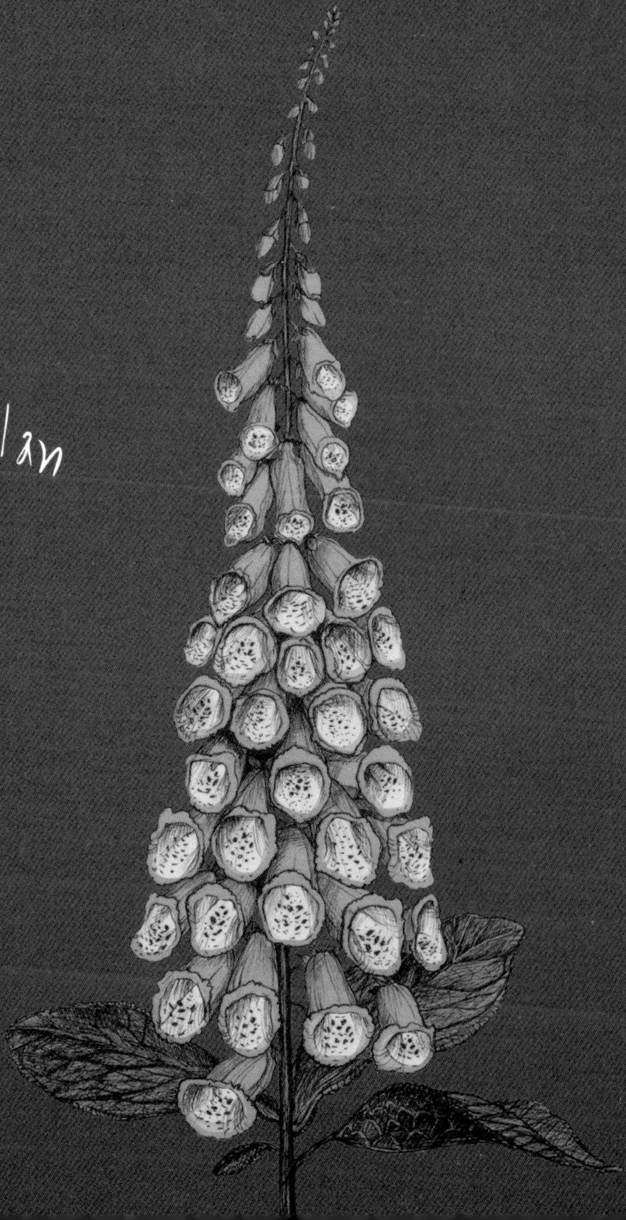

The pansy! A word used by friend and foe

Was clearly the botanical way to go

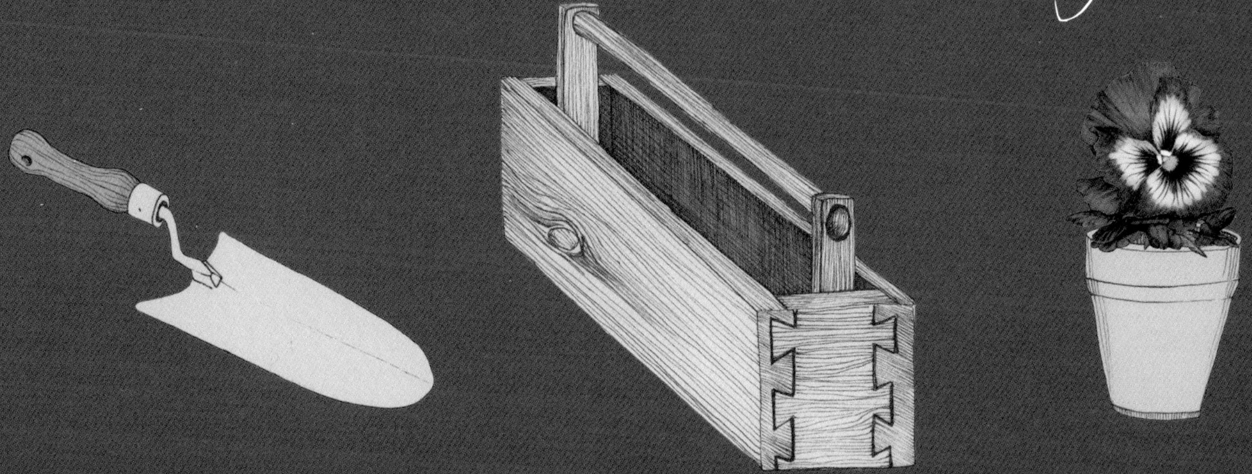

At every place where he'd been hurt

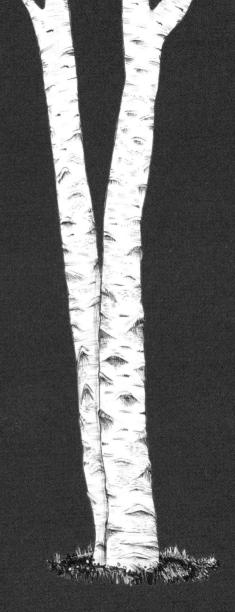

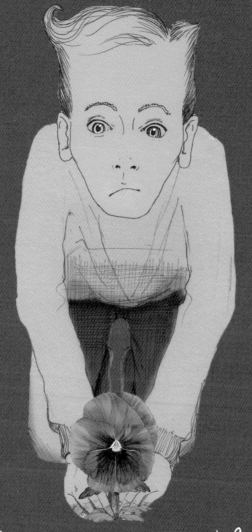

He planted pansies in the dirt

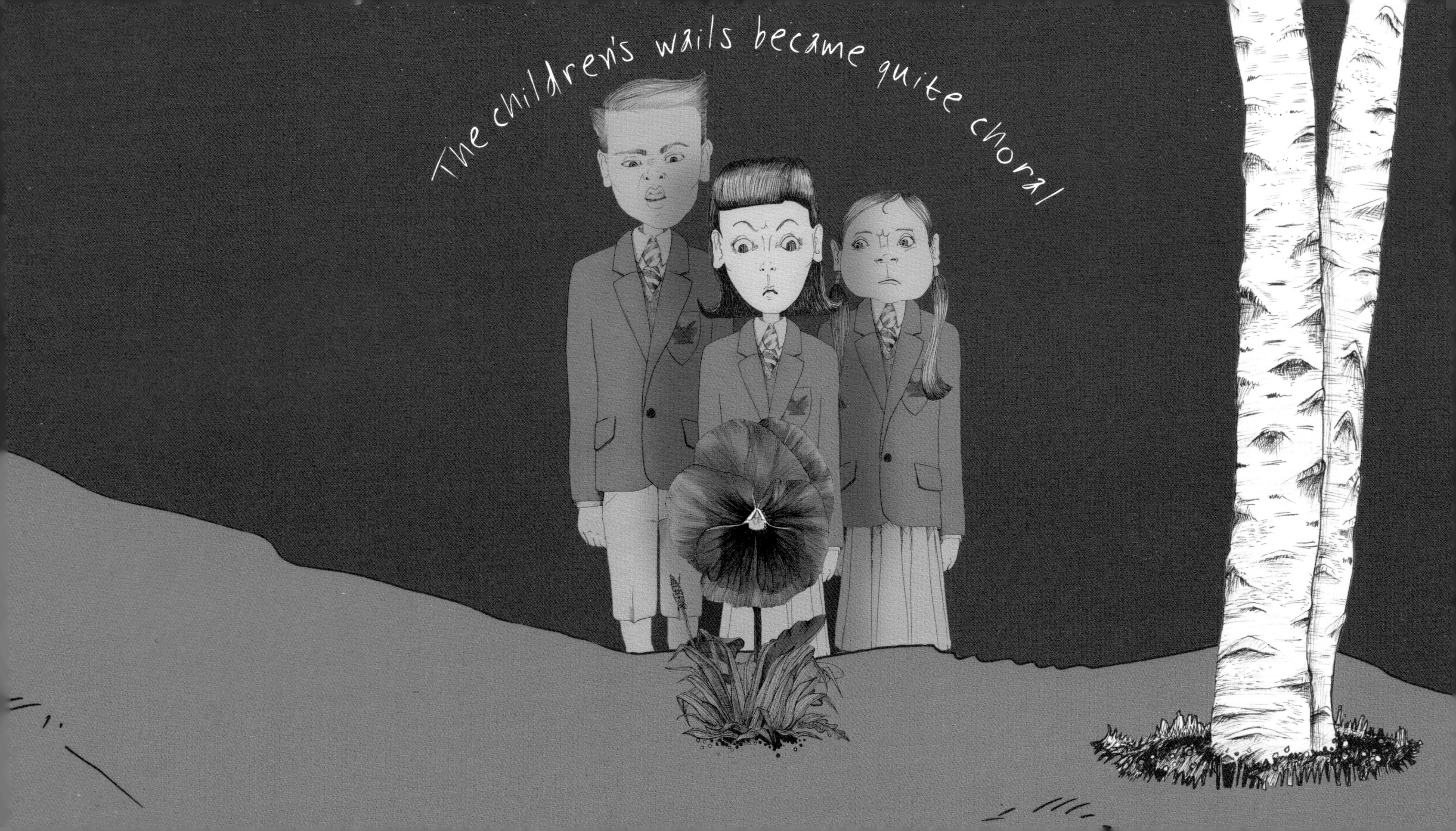
The children's wails became quite choral

"Who has turned our schoolyard floral?"

He explained the motive for this caper, by writing in a dart of paper

The plane took flight and came to land, within the reach of a teacher's hand

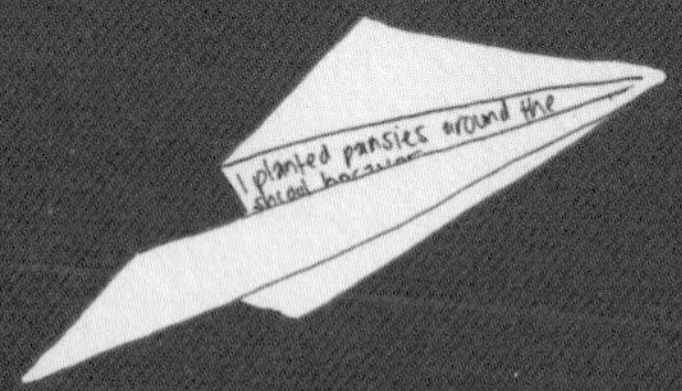
I planted pansies around the

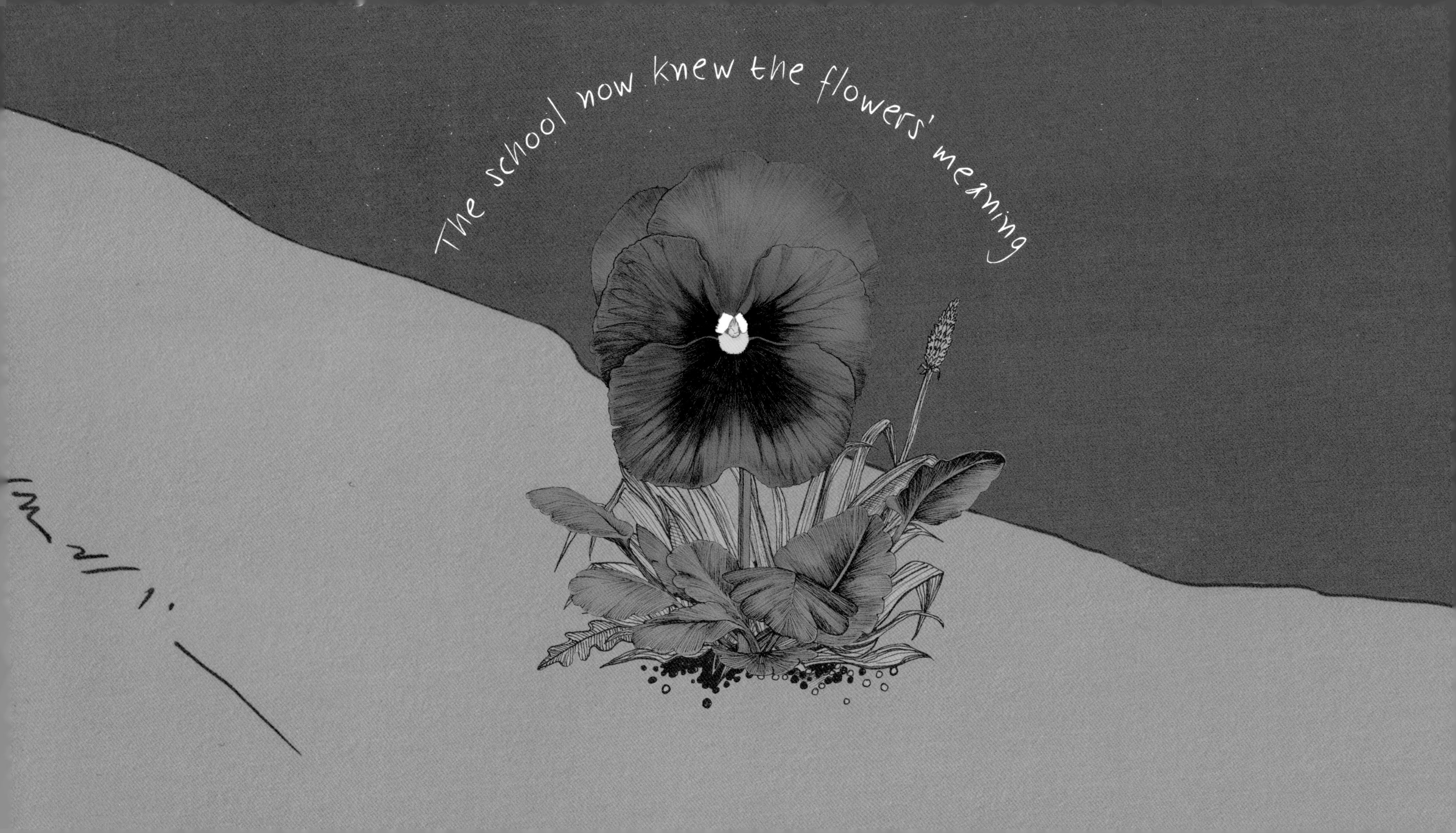
The school now knew the flowers' meaning

And wasted no time intervening

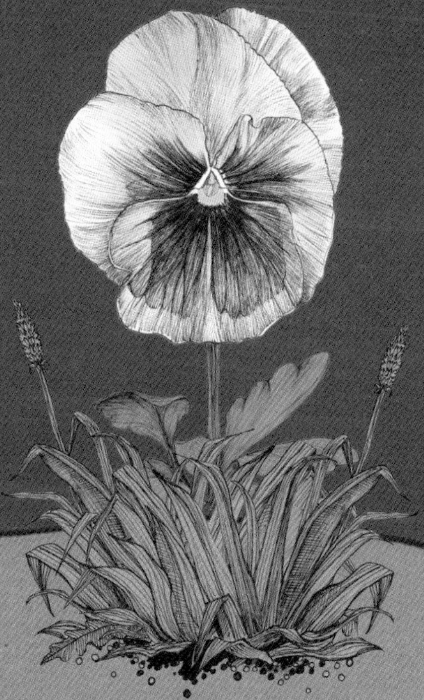

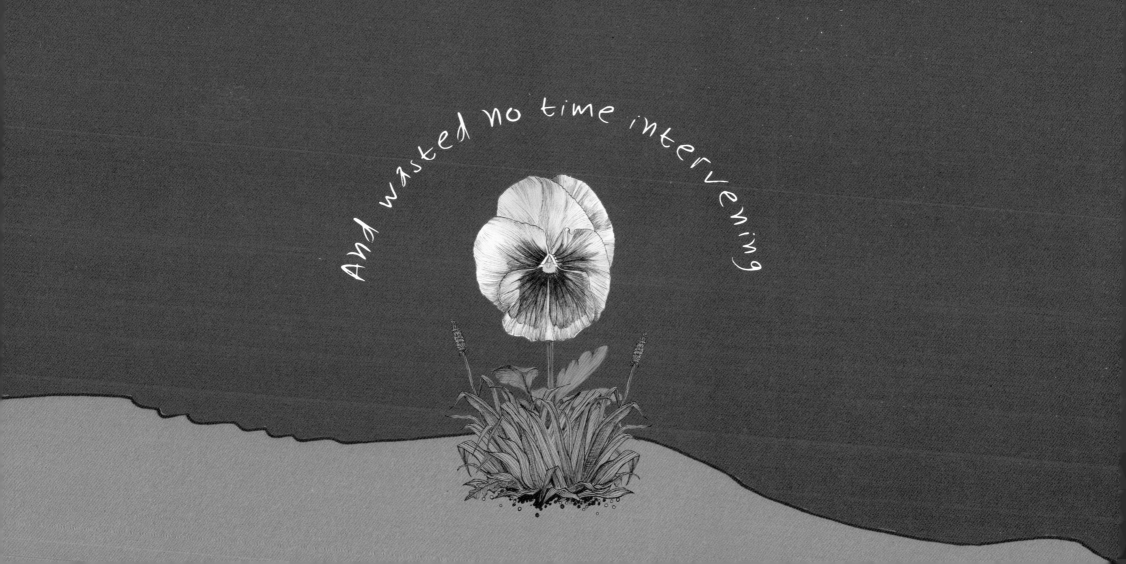

They kept offenders after school
until they learned the golden rule

That everybody has the right
To live without the need to fight

Now fewer words of hate were said, he no longer felt a sense of dread

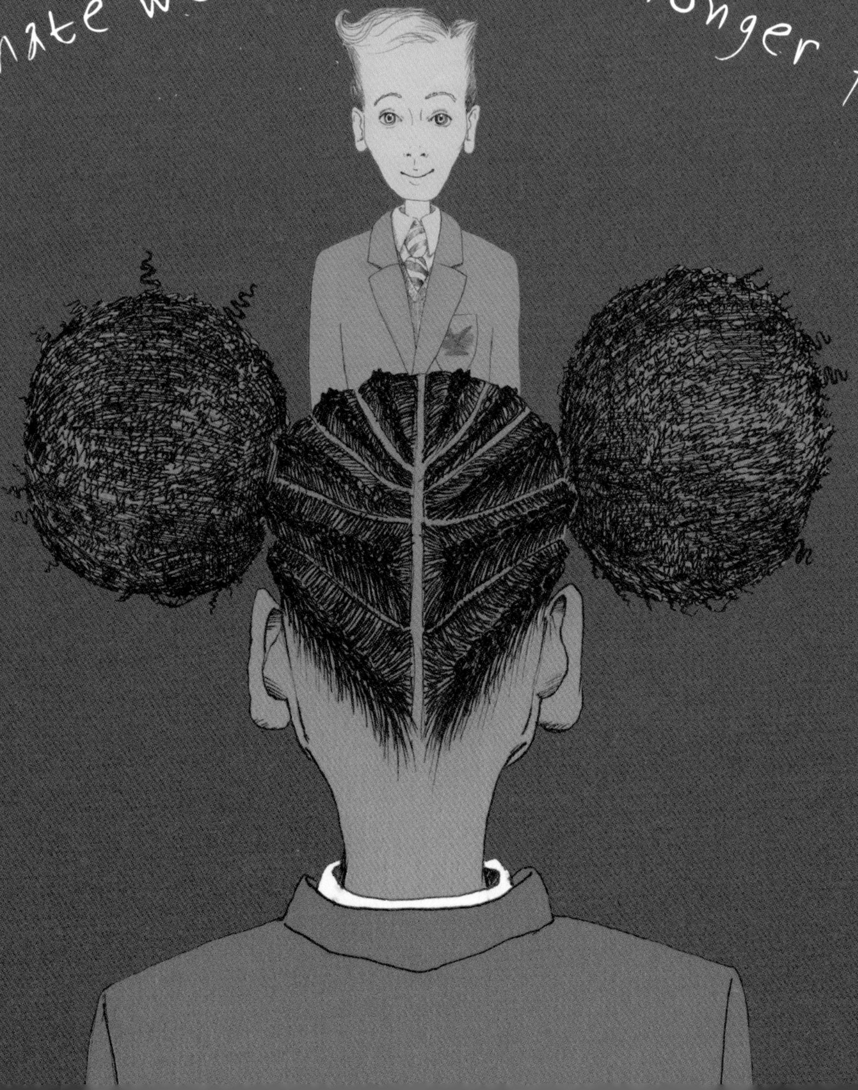

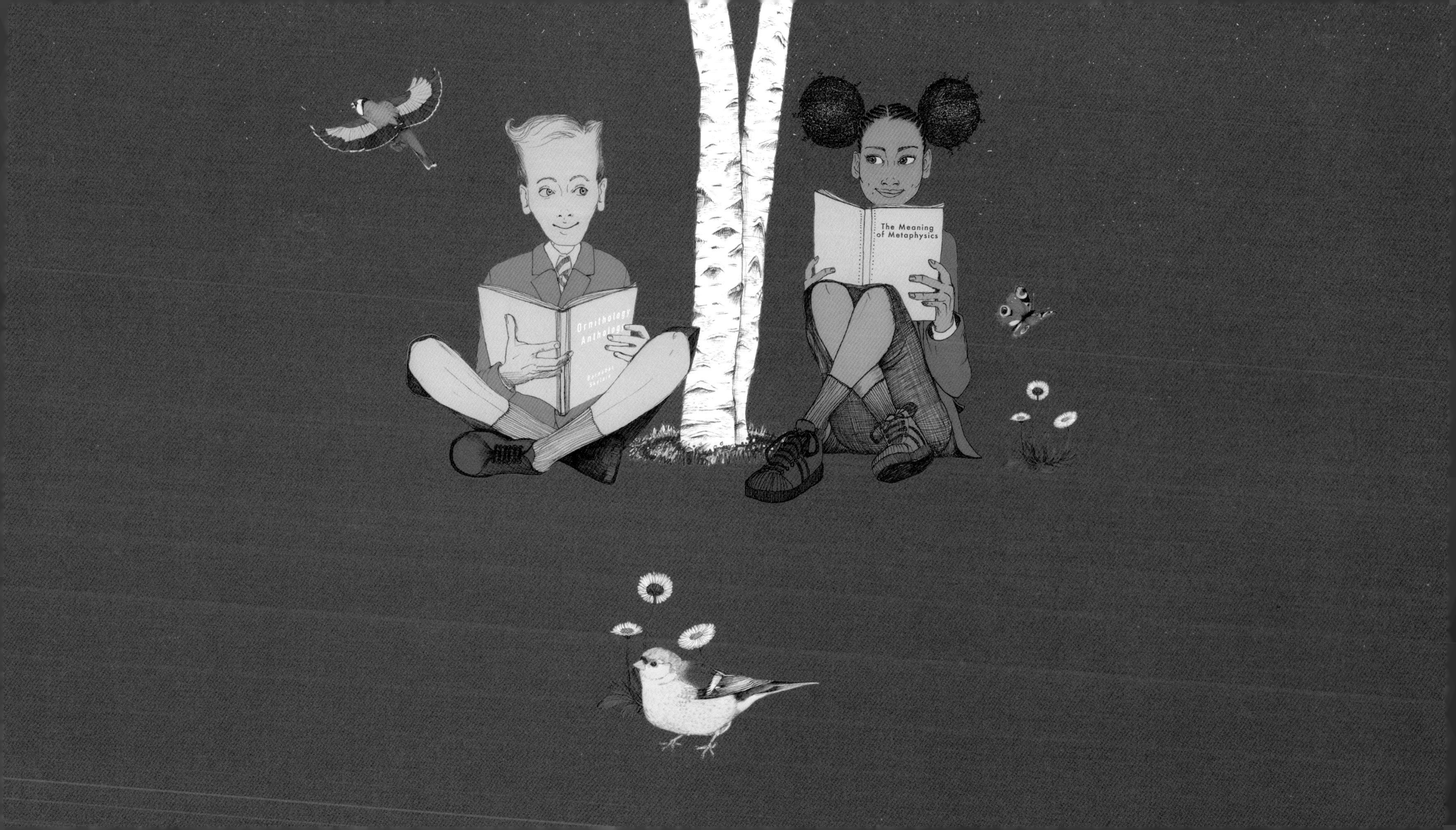

Ornithology Anthology
The Meaning of Metaphysics

His modest plan to raise awareness, increased the prospect of future fairness

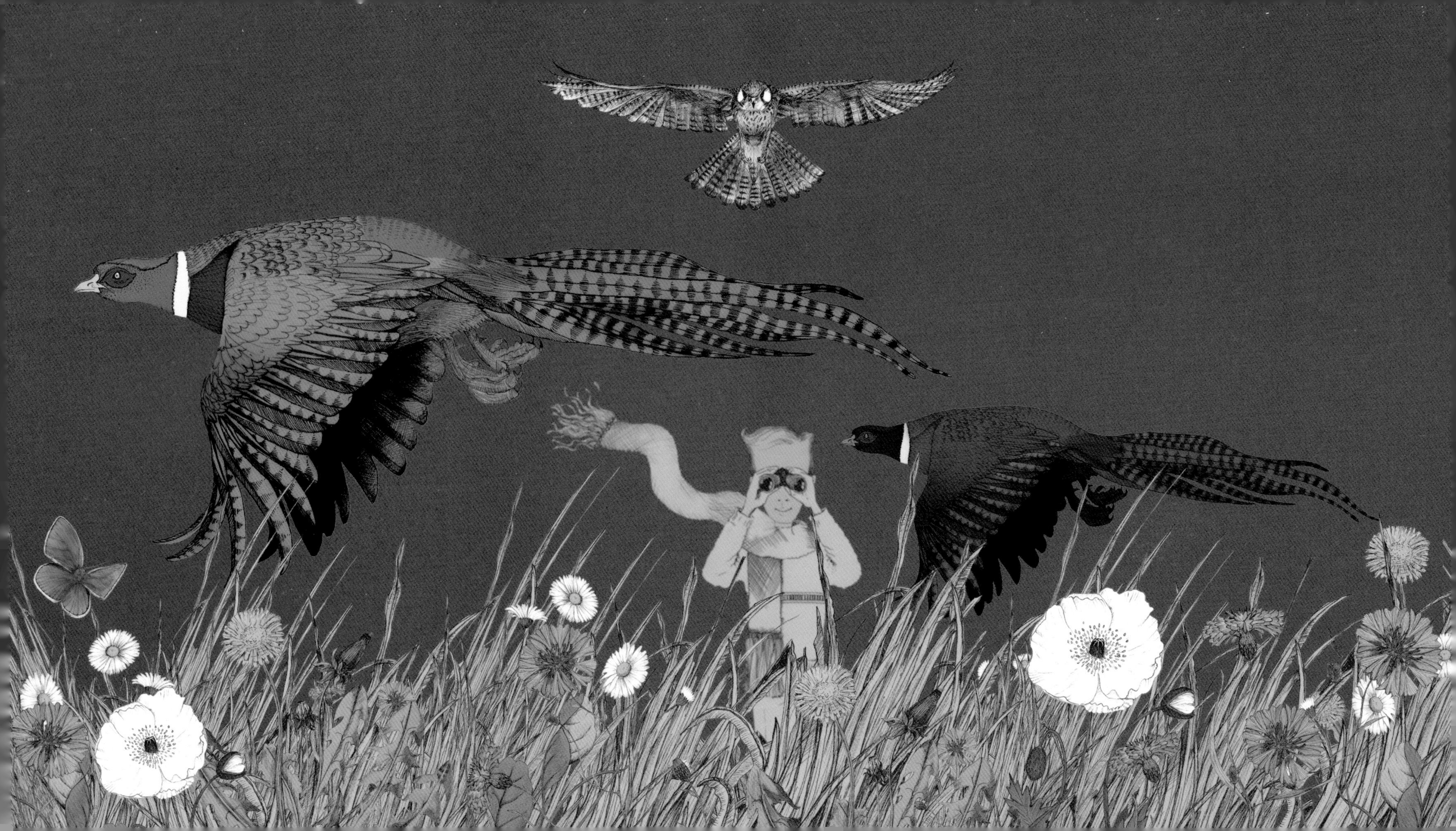

He returned to gaze at the birds above
And felt nothing but awe and love.

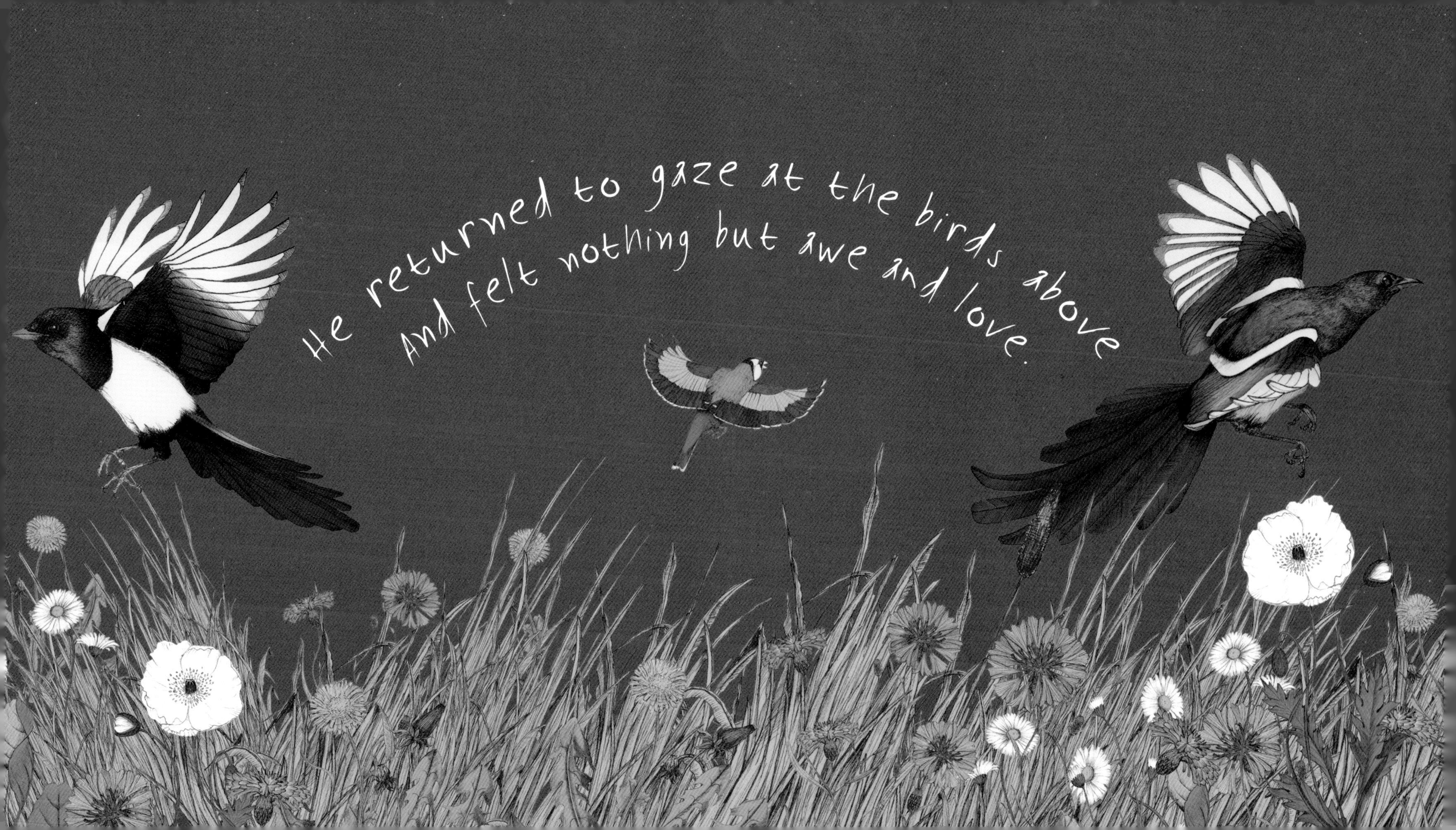

Field Notes

Field Notes are used by naturalists to take notes on the flora and fauna they find on their expeditions.

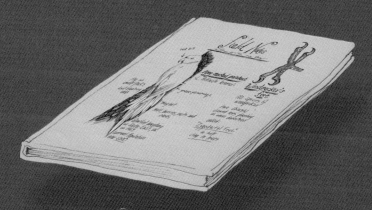

The Language of Flowers

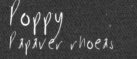

Poppy
Papaver rhoeas

The poppy became associated with remembering fallen soldiers due to its presence in the fields of France during the First World War.

Cornflower
Centaurea cyanus

In France the cornflower is similar to the poppy and is associated with war veterans. During the one hundredth anniversary of the Battle of the Somme in 2016, cornflower and poppy petals fell over the Thiepval Memorial in Authuille, France.

Bluebell
Hyacinthoides Nonscripta

The bluebell is common in the woods of England. They bloom in early spring creating carpets of blue so intense a blue hue appears to hang low over the woodland floor.

Snowdrop
Galanthus nivalis

The current symbolism of the snowdrop is generally positive, signifying hope, rebirth and the end of winter. However in Victorian England a single snowdrop was considered an omen of death.

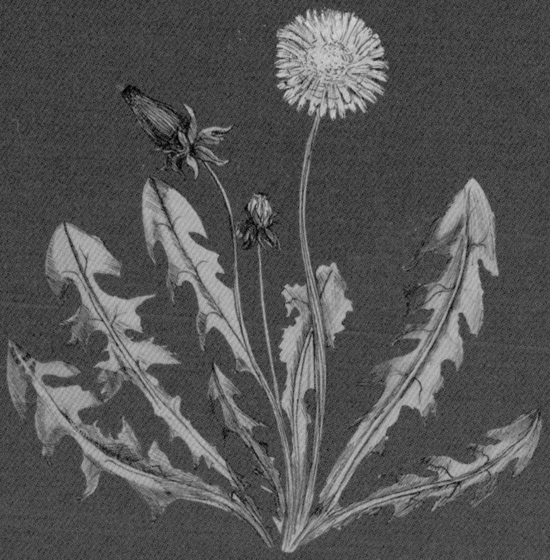

Dandelion

Taraxacum officinale

Various alternative names of the dandelion refer to wetting the bed, including the French 'pissenlit'. This is apparently due to the strong diuretic effect of the plants root.

Foxglove

Digitalis

It is said that the foxglove's name comes from 'folks' gloves', with 'folk' referring to fairy folk. It is said that picking a foxglove offends the fairies.

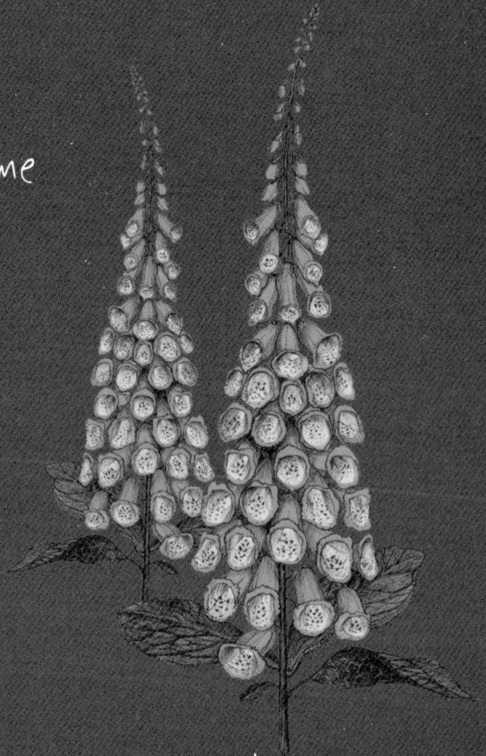

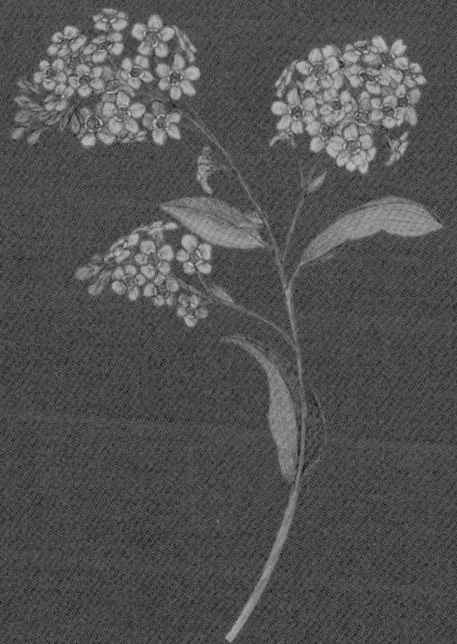

Forget me not

Myosotis arvensis

The forget me not's unusual name is associated with many tales of love and remembrance and has been written about by many esteemed poets, including Keats.

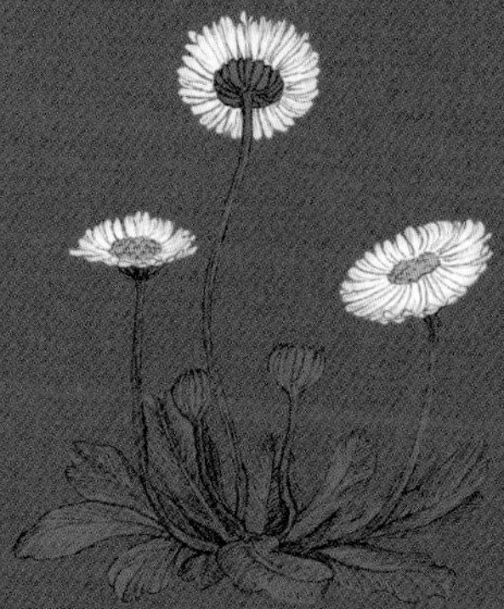

Daisy

Bellis perennis

The daisy's name is thought to derive from the old English 'daes eag' and originates from 'days eye' after the way in which the flower opens its petals at dawn, like an eye.

Pansy

Viola tricolor

The word pansy comes from the French word 'penser', meaning to think or ponder.

It's thought that men who were considered overly thoughtful, were weak and became associated with the flower. Pansy became a derogatory term of abuse for effeminate men or boys in the twentieth century. Despite the association with weakness, pansies are very tough and can survive winter frosts.

Notes on Birds

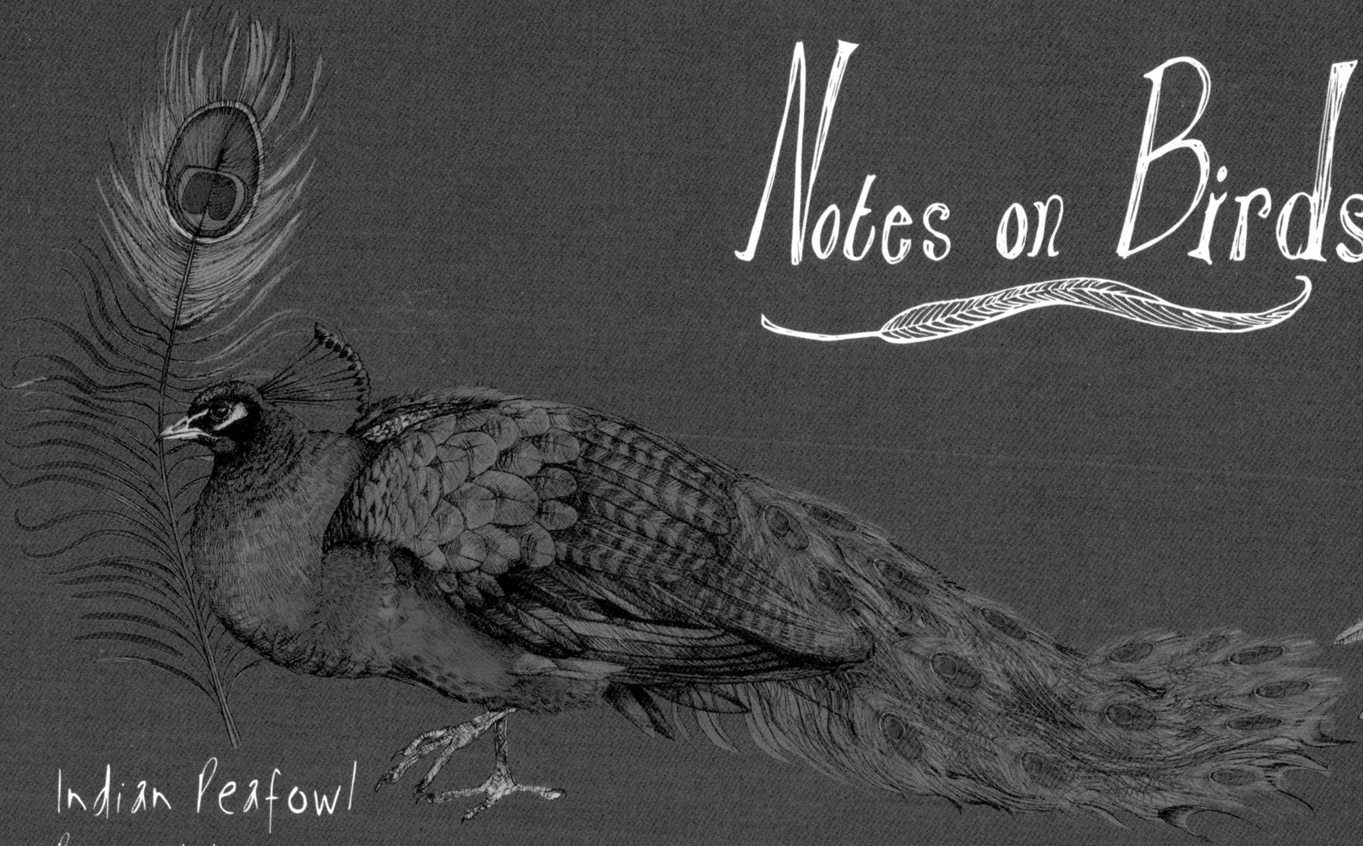

Indian Peafowl

Pavo cristatus

Often known as the peacock, this refers to the more colourful male of the species. Imported from the Indian subcontinent to decorate European parkland. The peacock displays its large train and makes its loud call, 'mayawe' to attract the less colourful female peahen. The peafowls call is also stimulated by the sound of thunder.

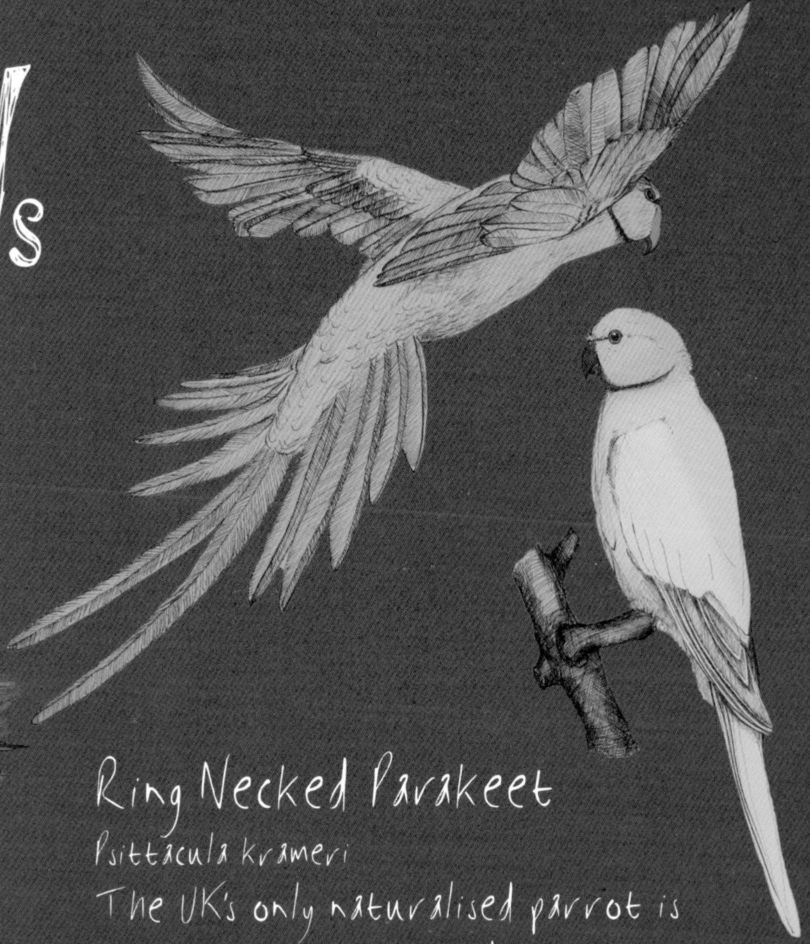

Ring Necked Parakeet

Psittacula krameri

The UK's only naturalised parrot is thought to have escaped from captivity in the nineteen seventies. It is very loud and often roosts in large flocks.

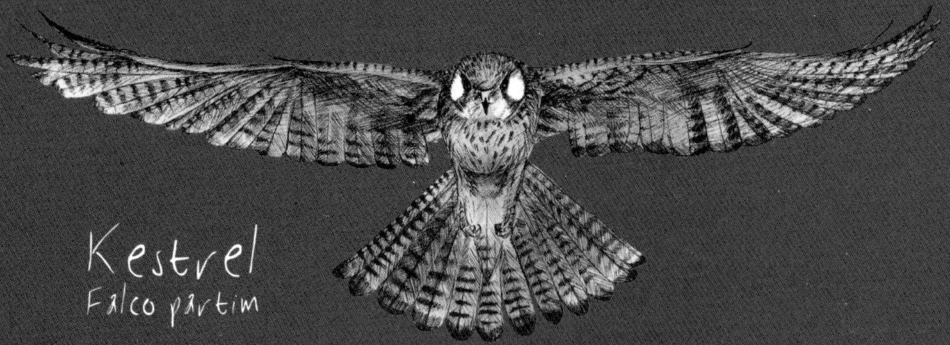

Kestrel

Falco partim

Kestrels are found in a wide variety of habitats, from moor and heath, to farmland and urban areas. They can often be seen hovering over fields hunting for prey.

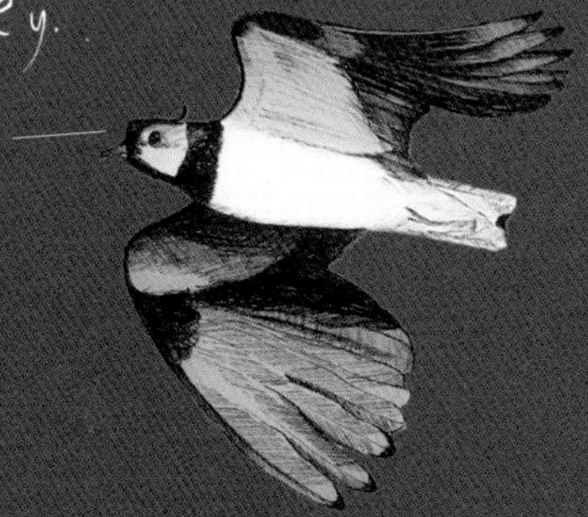

Lapwing

Vanellus vanellus

Also known as the peewit, after its call, its proper name describes its wavering flight. Its black and white appearance and round winged shape in flight make it very distintive.

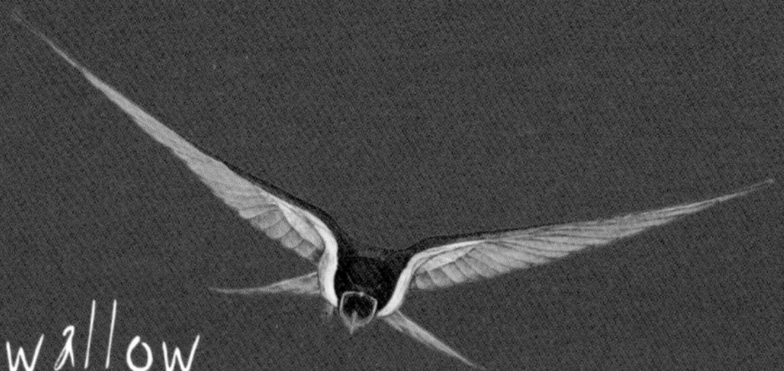

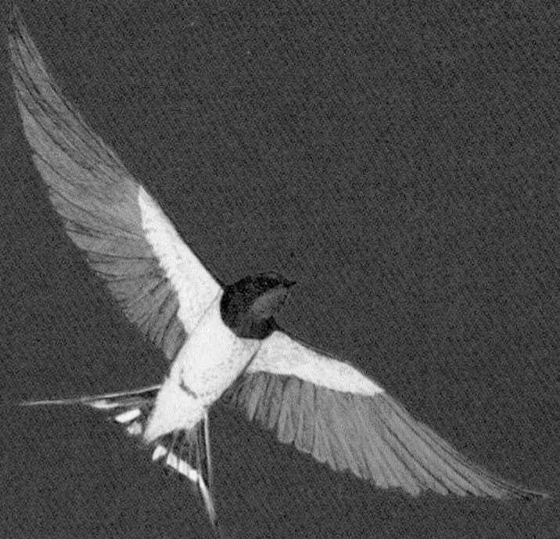

Swallow

Hirundo rustica

Swallows are extremely agile in flight and spend most of their time on the wing. They're migrating birds, appearing in Britain in the summer months.

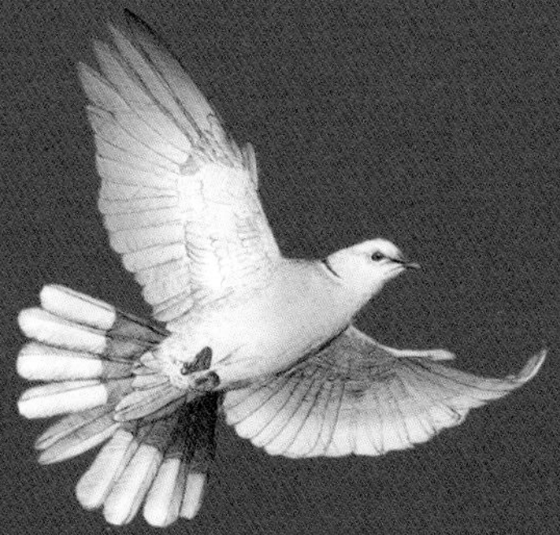

Collared Dove

Streptopelia decaocto

Collared doves are known for their monotonous cooing. They only started appearing in the United Kingdom in the fifties. They have since colonised the entire country.

Pheasant
Phasianus colchicus

Pheasants were introduced into Britain for the wealthy to shoot. They have since colonised fields and farmland across the country.

Goldfinch and Chaffinch
Carduelis carduelis and Fringilla coelebs

Finches are amongst the most colourful garden birds in Britain. The goldfinch has yellow wing markings and a red face. The male chaffinch has a bright pink breast, the female has more subtle hues.

Magpie
Pica pica

This common member of the crow family is known by the famous rhyme. One for sorrow, two for joy. Three for a girl, four for a boy, five for silver, six for gold, seven for a secret never to be told. Eight for a wish, nine for a kiss, ten for a marriage never to be old.

Starling
Sturnus vulgaris

Starlings are one of the most common garden birds. They often form large roosts at dusk, flying in large undulating flocks known as murmurations.

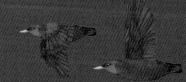

the pansy project

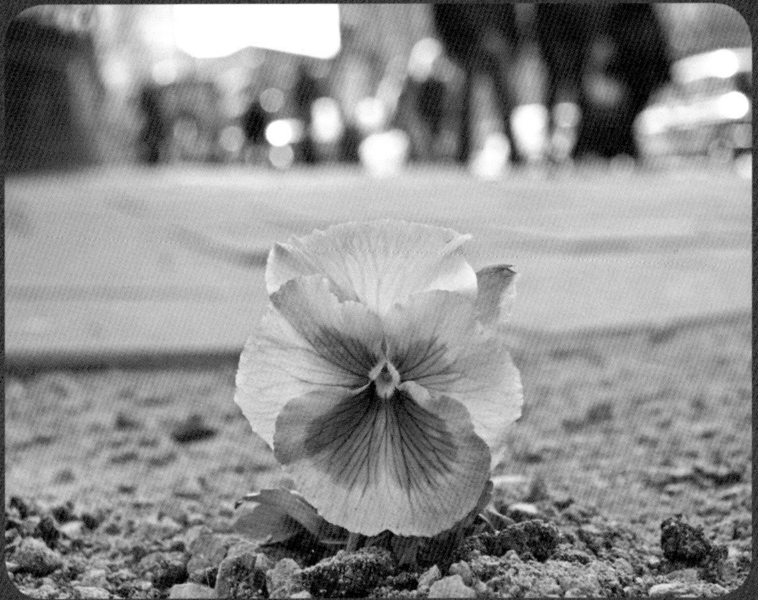

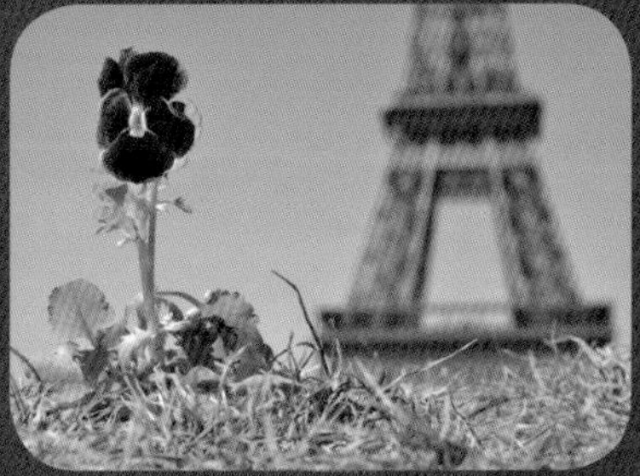

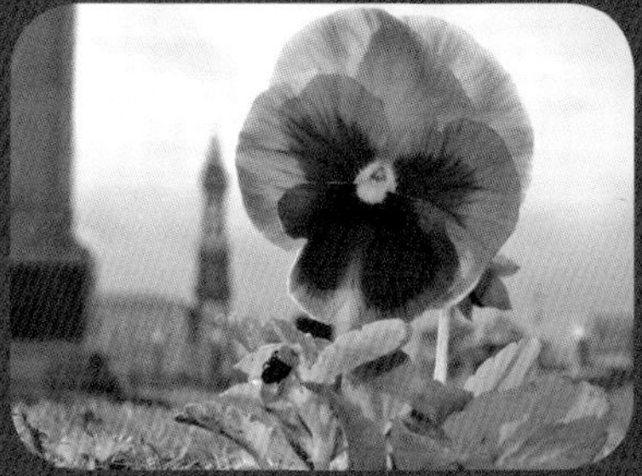

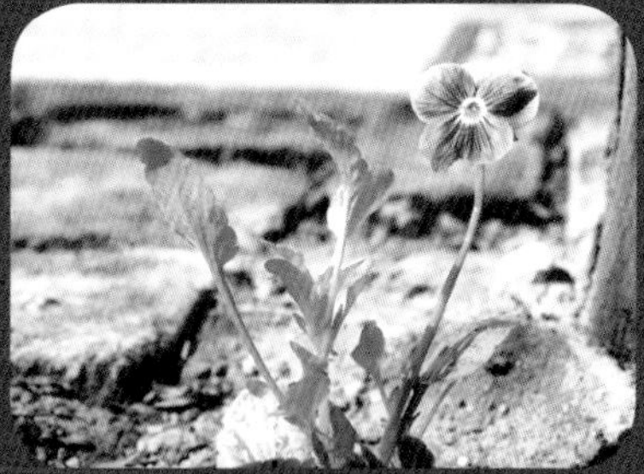

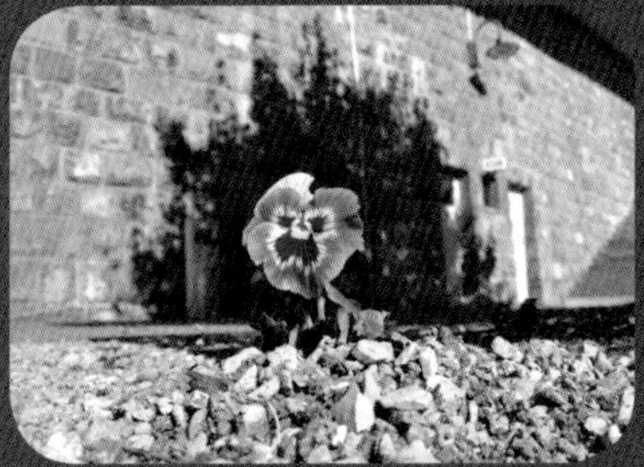

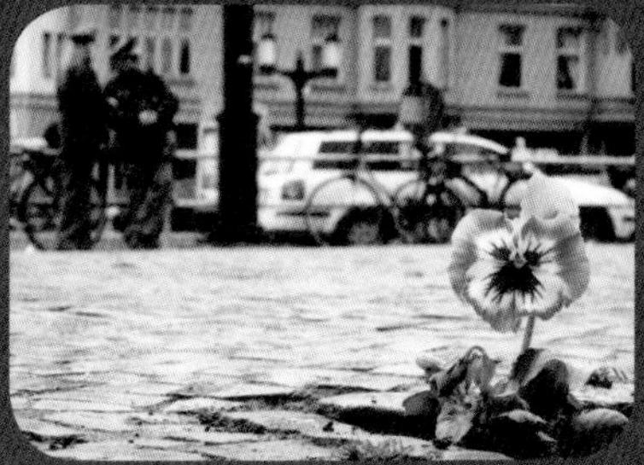

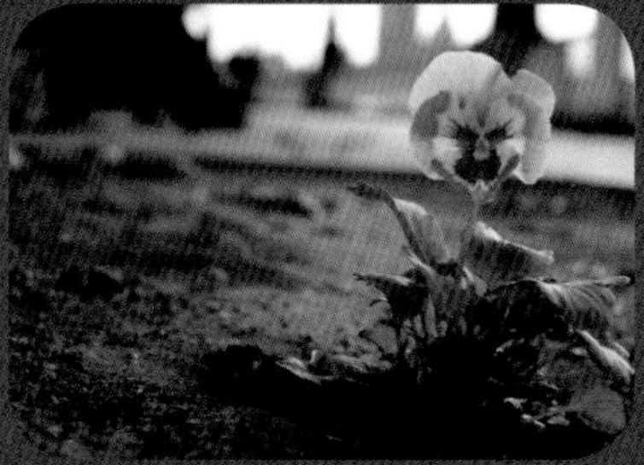

Above: 'Batty!' Kings Cross, London. Followed by pansies planted in Paris, Blackpool, New York, Geneva, Berlin and London.

Pansy Boy is a fictionalised origin story of The Pansy Project. The Pansy Project was devised by Paul Harfleet in 2005. Since then Harfleet has planted pansies at the sites of homophobia around the world. For more information on The Pansy Project visit: www.thepansyproject.com.

Above: Paul Harfleet (left) aged 10, looking through binoculars alongside his mother (Theone) and siblings (James and Jane).

As a child Paul was a keen young ornitholigist and loved examining illustrations of the birds that surrounded him in the South East of England.

Thank you Charlie, Grandad & Jenny and my mum. And thank you to my friends and family who helped along the way.

First published in Great Britain by Barbican Press in 2017
Copyright © Paul Harfleet 2017
Barbican Press, Hull.
Registered office: 1 Ashenden Road, London E5 0DP
www.barbicanpress.com

@barbicanpress1
A CIP catalogue for this book is available from the British Library
ISBN: 978-1-909954-24-3

Printed in India